D1449965

the photographic guide to
exposure

the photographic guide to

exposure

Chris Weston

Photographers' Institute Press

First published 2004 by
Photographers' Institute Press / PIP,
166 High Street, Lewes,
East Sussex, BN7 1XU

ISBN 1 86108 387 4

A catalogue record of this book is available from the British Library.

Publisher: Paul Richardson
Art Director: Ian Smith
Production Manager: Stuart Poole
Managing Editor: Gerrie Purcell
Commissioning Editor: April McCroskie
Editor: James Beattie
Designer: Chris Halls, Mind's Eye Design Ltd, Lewes
Artwork: John Yates (pages 18, 32, 53, 56, 61, 64, 72, 78, 79, 82, 83, 86 and 124);
Chris Halls (pages 85, 106, 108 and 104) and Gilda Pacitti (page 34)
Typefaces: Avenir, GillSans and Meridien
Colour origination by Icon Reproduction, UK
Printed and bound by Kyodo Printing (Singapore)

ACKNOWLEDGEMENTS

I often wonder how many people take the time to read the acknowledgements given in books. I know I am as guilty as any in often skipping this page, eager to get to the main content inside. So I ask, please spare a moment for the following people because without them this book would not exist:

The entire team at Photographers' Institute Press for the late nights, long hours and weekends spent toiling over my notes; to Ann and John in South Africa, David in New Zealand, and Chris in Seattle without whom many of these pictures would not have been taken; to Jane and Jim at Intro2020 for the warm welcome I always receive when begging for the use of equipment; Steve and Guy at Bowens International for their thoughts, ideas and, most importantly, for their time. I would also like to pass on my gratitude to those people who dedicate their lives to the protection of many of the animals that I photograph for a living. In particular to Peter at Santago and to everyone at the English School of Falconry, whose creatures appear in this book. And finally, to my darling wife who, beyond any reason I can imagine, still puts up with me after all these years. Once again, I am indebted to you all.

DEDICATION

This book is dedicated to the photographers and writers, journalists and presenters, biologists and ecologists whose love of nature continues to inspire me.

Introduction

One of the questions I am asked most often on workshops and at seminars is, 'How do I get an accurate exposure?' Exposure is one of the fundamentals of the photographic art and yet it remains one of the most mysterious and seemingly complicated aspects of photographic technique. Similarly, the seemingly simple question posed above is one of the most difficult to answer. For, while the process of image capture is based on science, photographic exposure is open to artistic interpretation. What one photographer considers an accurate exposure, in that it captures the mood or essence of a scene as he or she saw it, another may consider inaccurate because it fails to conform to pre-defined technical rules.

◀ *Light, time of day and weather together pose questions about correct exposure.*

Lake Mathesson, South Island, New Zealand.

35mm camera, 50mm lens, Fuji Velvia, 1/20sec at f/22

In dealing with the subject of exposure it is as important to illustrate how to control exposure, as it is to explain how to calculate it. Modern cameras, with all their electronic wizardry and computer microchips, have made the technical aspects of exposure much simpler for everyone. What all cameras fail to achieve, however, is an appreciation for the artistry of the person behind the lens. When you point a camera towards a scene it doesn't see what you see it merely provides a means of recording what you see using silver or pixel. The role played by the camera is no more than that of vacuous observer, and it will give vacuous results without artistic direction from you.

So what am I saying? I'm saying that in reality there is no such thing as correct exposure and that what we are all striving for in the pictures we make is faithful exposure. An exposure that accurately depicts the scene we saw in our mind's eye and echoes the inner passion that led us to make the photograph at all. The purpose of this book is to provide you with not just another manual on the technicalities of exposure, it is also a guide to controlling exposure as a means of recording your emotional responses to any given scene or subject. That means that this book will only be effective with input from you. For me to answer truthfully the question, 'How do I get an accurate exposure?' is contingent on you knowing what effect you are trying to achieve.

◄ *Photographic exposure is open to individual interpretation. There is no such thing as correct exposure, merely one faithful to the vision of the photographer when he/she fired the shutter.*

35mm camera, 100mm lens, Fuji Velvia, 1/60sec at f/5.6

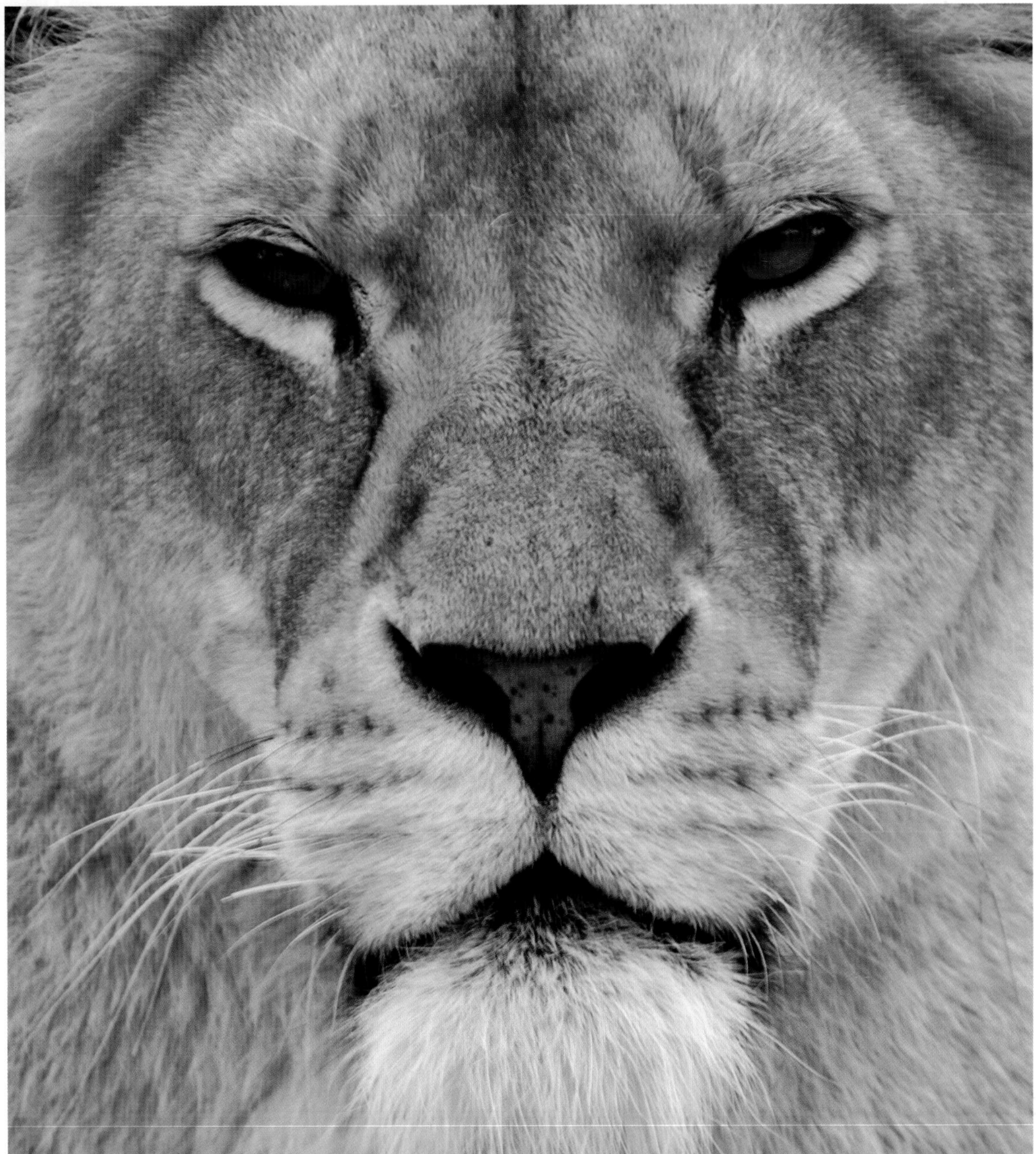

▲ *Lioness (controlled conditions)*

Photography is the art of managing light and manipulating the elements of design to communicate personal vision. Mastering these disciplines is your route to producing consistently compelling images.

To help you along the way I have split the book into three main elements. Firstly, I will guide you through the basic principles of exposure and identify the mechanisms by which you can control it. Next I discuss how to interpret the data provided by the light meter and how to moderate that data to achieve an image that accurately reflects your vision. Finally, using case studies I will demonstrate how to take the information contained in the first two sections and put it into practice in the real world. Because of the nature of the book, and its intended audience, I have made certain assumptions. Firstly, the aim is that you obtain sufficient knowledge to allow you to control the functions of your camera that relate to exposure. This means that you must use a camera that allows you to control these basic functions. It should allow manual adjustment of lens aperture, shutter speed and ISO or ISO equivalency rating. Second, I have written this book to enable faithful exposures in-camera. Therefore, *Chapter 7: Post camera exposure control* is intended as an overview of exposure adjustments that can be made once the image has been created. Finally, because the majority of photographers today shoot in colour, the emphasis of the book is in exposing photographs shot in colour. That said, the guiding principle throughout is to impart sufficient knowledge, beyond that of complex tables and indecipherable logarithms, to allow you to determine faithful exposure settings when you need them most, that is when you're out in the field or in the studio.

Of course, you may disagree with some of my observations. I encourage you to question my interpretations because by doing so you will become better placed to question your own decisions and selections and, through informed reasoning, become the master of your camera, rather than it's slave. As the photographer it is your job to manage the camera in such a way that it captures your photographic imagination. Your knowledge and understanding of light, the nuances of film and the limitations of the light meter, together with an appreciation of your own photographic purpose and direction will open your eyes to the secrets of attaining consistent, faithful exposures. As the author of this book it is my job now to teach you how.

▼ *The subjectivity of exposure should lead you to ask yourself, 'How would I have photographed that scene differently?' By challenging your perception in this way you will soon begin to master your camera and take control of the images it creates.*

35mm panoramic camera, 45mm lens, Fuji Velvia, 1/6sec at f/16

Understanding exposure control

Ever since the French lithographer and inventor, Nicéphore Niépce, discovered that by coating a pewter plate with asphaltum a permanent image could be retained, controlling exposure has been one of the fundamental disciplines of photography. Despite the ever-increasing sophistication of camera design and technology, and changes in the materials used for image capture, the three principal mechanisms for controlling exposure remain unchanged. Controlling the sensitivity of the material, the amount of light reaching that material, and the length of the exposure is just as vital now as it has been throughout the history of photography.

◀ *The fine mist and reflections of Alnwick Castle in Northumberland, England, combine to create a timeless image.*

35mm camera, 24mm lens, Fuji Velvia, 1/30sec at f/22

The dictionary describes photography as, 'the process of recording images on sensitized material by the action of light'. How faithfully the image is recorded, in terms of hue, colour and contrast, depends on three things:

1. The **sensitivity** of the material
2. The **amount** of light reaching the sensitized material
3. The **length of time** the sensitized material is exposed to the light

Too little light and/or too short a time will result in underexposure – a dull, dark image lacking detail in shadow areas. On the other hand, too much light and/or too long a time will result in overexposure – a washed out image lacking detail in highlight areas. The trick is to get just the right amount of light for the correct length of time, given the sensitivity of the material, to record the scene as you interpret it.

To achieve faithful exposure the camera provides you with three basic controls:

1. ISO (ISO equivalency) rating
2. Lens aperture
3. Shutter speed

All three controls can be adjusted independently. However, each is interdependent on the others and understanding their relationship is the basis for understanding exposure control.

The standard measurement for exposure is the stop. Any change in ISO rating, lens aperture or shutter speed is referred to as an *n* stop change, where *n* equals the degree of change.

For example an ISO 200 film is referred to as being one-stop faster than an ISO 100 film; a change in lens aperture from f/5.6 to f/8 is considered a one stop change in lens aperture; and an increase in shutter speed from 1/125sec to 1/250sec is considered to be a one-stop change in shutter speed.

▼ *In this image, taken in Westland/Tai Poutini National Park in New Zealand, the key was to balance the highlights, with the dark shadows to give the scene a three-dimensional form.*

35mm panoramic camera, 45mm lens, Fuji Velvia, 1/30sec at f/16

ISO (ISO equivalency) rating

Table 1 – ISO rating						
	Slow		Medium		Fast	
ISO rating	50	100	200	400	800	1600

▲ *The ISO rating is a standard measurement of film/PS sensitivity to light. Films with a low rating (50–100 ISO) are considered slow because they take longer to react to light than medium-speed films (200–400 ISO) and fast films (800–1600 ISO) which react very quickly.*

The ISO (International Standards Organisation) rating – sometimes referred to as the ASA (American Standards Association) rating, which it replaced – is the standardized measure of a film's sensitivity to light. A film with a low ISO rating, such as Fuji Velvia 50 or Kodachrome 64, is less sensitive to light than a film with a higher ISO number. In practical terms this means a low ISO film needs either brighter light or a longer period of time, for a correctly exposed image to form on it, than a film with a higher ISO rating would need. Such low ISO films are often referred to as 'slow' films.

Every subsequent doubling in the sensitivity – 'speed' – of the film (e.g. ISO 100, ISO 200, ISO 400, ISO 800, etc.) halves the brightness of light or the length of time required for an image to form. The ISO rating of the film, therefore, affects the exposure by determining how quickly a film reacts to light.

All films are given an ISO rating by the manufacturer. However, it is possible to alter the given rating of a film by changing the film speed setting on the camera. What affect this has on exposure and the final image, and why you might choose to do it will be discussed later in the book (see page 71).

In digital capture, where film is replaced with a photo-sensor (PS), such as a CCD (charge-coupled device) or CMOS (Complementary Metal Oxide Sensor), the sensitivity of the photo sensor is measured in the same way and with the same units as it is for film. A sensor's sensitivity is referred to as its ISO equivalency. Therefore, a PS set to an ISO equivalency of 200, for example, will react to light in much the same way as the same ISO speed film would.

Lens aperture

The lens aperture controls the amount of light reaching the film/PS. In isolation it works in the same way as the pupil in a human eye. In very bright conditions the pupil contracts, as it needs less light to distinguish detail. In very dark conditions the pupil gets bigger because it needs to let in more light to distinguish detail. Changing the size of the lens aperture, then, allows you to decide how much light is to reach the film.

All camera lenses are calibrated to the same scale of measurement known as f/stops. These can be seen on the lens aperture ring and are shown in the LCD panels of modern cameras. The range of f/stop numbers varies depending on the lens but always forms part of the same scale, illustrated in the table below. Typically they will start at around f/1.4 and go up to around f/45.

In practical terms f/stops are simply a mark of measurement, but their original and indeed their name refers to the relationship between the effective focal length of the lens and the diameter of the aperture. f/2 means the diameter is half the effective focal length of the lens; f/4 a quarter. The larger the f/stop number the smaller the lens aperture, as depicted in the illustration below. Increasing the aperture by one full stop will double the amount of light reaching the film. Reducing the aperture by one full stop will halve the amount of light reaching the film.

Controlling exposure via lens aperture will affect depth of field. The larger the aperture (small f/stop numbers) the less depth of field you will have to work with, while reducing the aperture (large f/stop numbers) will increase the available depth of field. This will impact on how a scene appears in the final image, which must be taken into account when setting your exposure values relative to your composition (see chapter 4).

Table 2 – f/stop index

f/1.4	f/2	f/2.8	f/4	f/5.6	f/8	f/11	f/16	f/22	f/32	f/45

▼ *Lens aperture is determined by the size of the hole through which light passes. Smaller apertures, denoted by the larger f/numbers (f/16, f/22, f/32, etc.), give the greatest depth of field, while large apertures, denoted by small f/numbers (f/2, f/2.8. f/4, etc.), produce limited depth of field.*

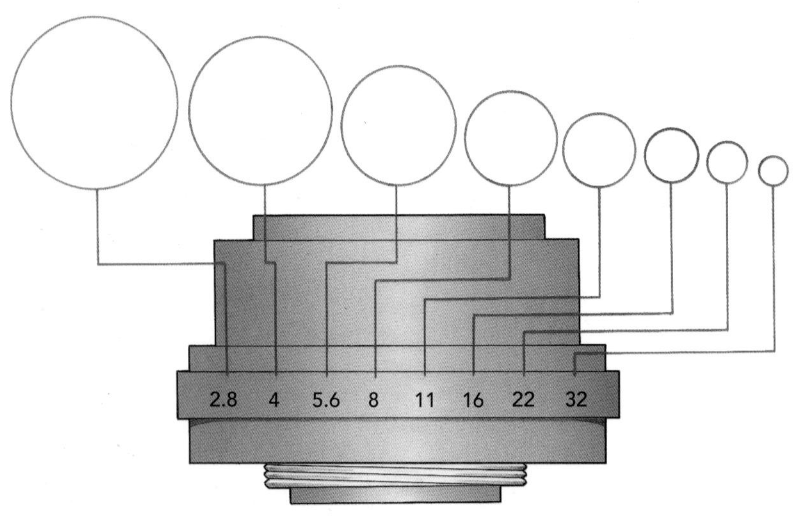

▶ *Lens aperture is one of the principal determinants of depth of field. In the top image a small aperture of f/32 gives enough depth of field to render the whole bridge sharp.*

▶ *In the bottom image the aperture has been set to f/4. The wider aperture has resulted in a loss of depth of field which has led to a loss of sharpness.*

Working with lens aperture and shutter speed

Why take the trouble to set apertures and shutter speeds yourself? Why not just let your camera select the appropriate exposure settings? The answer to this question lies in photographic composition. The lens aperture and shutter speed settings you use can completely change the way the subject is rendered in the final image. Lens aperture, which controls depth of field, can help to include or isolate areas of foreground and background, either focusing attention on the main subject, by placing it in isolation, or creating a sense of place by positioning it within a broader context by including the foreground and background. Shutter speed defines the appearance of motion. A fast shutter speed will freeze motion keeping the subject sharp with well-defined edges to the details, though this may give the subject a static appearance. A slow shutter speed, on the other hand, will blur motion giving the subject less well-defined details and adding strong visual energy to your photographs. Again this is an area where there is no right or wrong, so experiment.

Shutter speed

The final controlling factor in the exposure equation is shutter speed. Shutter speed defines the length of time any amount of light falls on the film/PS and is measured in fractions of seconds. Most cameras have pre-set shutter speeds between eight seconds and 1/1000sec, with an additional setting known as the bulb setting. In the bulb setting the shutter remains open so long as the shutter release is depressed and enables exposure times beyond the slowest pre-defined camera setting, up to several minutes, hours or even days! More sophisticated modern cameras have a greater range of shutter speeds, as fast as 1/16,000sec at the time of writing.

As with lens aperture, a full one-stop change in shutter speed will either double or halve the length of time light passes through to the film/PS. For example, increasing the shutter speed from 1/125sec to 1/250sec will halve the length of time the shutter is open. Correspondingly, decreasing the shutter speed from 1/125sec to 1/60sec will double the length of time that the shutter is open.

Controlling exposure via shutter speed gives you control over how you depict movement in your images. A fast shutter speed, for example, will tend to freeze action, while a slow shutter speed will create blur, giving the subject a greater sense of motion.

▶ The shutter speed you choose will determine how motion is depicted in your photographs. Using a fast shutter speed (1/500sec) helped to freeze the action of these Cape buffalo as they stampeded up the riverbank away from predatory danger at their crossing point.

▼ *Unlike the buffalo, purposefully this image shows motion as a blur to heighten the emotional appeal of the photograph. A slow shutter speed of 1/15sec was used.*

Using all three controls together

The image above is underexposed. This has been corrected in the image below by using a slower shutter speed.

▲ *1/125sec at f/5.6 – ISO equivalency 200*
▼ *1/60sec at f/5.6 – ISO equivalency 200*

Setting faithful exposures requires an understanding of the relationship shared between the three different exposure controls and you working within their limitations to achieve the results you want.

When not enough light reaches the film/PS underexposure will occur. To rectify the situation you can either increase the lens aperture (known as, 'opening up the lens') or slow down the shutter speed. Either of these will have the effect of increasing the amount of light reaching the film/PS. Alternatively, and with increasing flexibility given digital capture technology, you can increase the sensitivity to light of the film/PS by increasing its ISO or ISO equivalency rating. This will cause the recording material to need less light in order to form an acceptable image.

When too much light is reaching the film/PS overexposure will result and you will need to reduce the level of light. This can be done by making the lens aperture smaller (bigger number) or by making the shutter speed faster. Again, you can alter the sensitivity of the film/PS to react more slowly to light, which will achieve the same aim. With film you can only alter the film speed for the whole film, whilst with digital cameras, it can be for individual frames.

Reciprocity law failure

When you use shutter speeds in excess of one second you begin to fall foul of reciprocity law failure.

The law of reciprocity states that any change in one exposure setting is off-set by an equal and opposite change in another. For example, an exposure of 1/125sec at f/8 will give the same results as 1/60sec at f/11. However, film, and to a lesser extent photo-sensors, become less sensitive to light the longer they are exposed. So, when shooting with shutter speeds greater than one second, you must allow more light in to make up for the loss in sensitivity. The table on page 104 gives guidelines for how this affects different films.

Once you have selected the appropriate combination of lens aperture and shutter speed relative to the sensitivity of the film/PS, any change in one will necessitate an equal and corresponding change in the other. For example, let's say that your correct exposure setting is 1/125sec at f/8. If you decide to alter the shutter speed to 1/250sec, thereby halving the time the light falls on the film, you will need to increase your aperture to f/5.6 (doubling the amount of light reaching the film) to maintain parity. Equally, if you were to decrease the aperture from f/8 to f/11, thereby halving the amount of light reaching the film, you would need to reduce your shutter speed from 1/125sec to 1/60sec – doubling the length of time that light affects the film/PS – in order to keep the overall exposure value consistent. The ability to change one of the exposure controls and compensate with a reciprocal change in another, whilst retaining the same overall level of exposure is known as the reciprocity law.

Letting in too much light for too long a time will result in your photographs appearing too bright and washed out, like the image on the facing page. Reducing the aperture or ISO rating of the film/PS, or increasing shutter speed will show more detail, as in the image below.

◀ *Image left: 1/30sec at f/5.6 – ISO equivalency 200*
▼ *Image below: 1/60sec at f/5.6 – ISO equivalency 200*

So, what this indicates is that exactly the same amount of light falls on the film or PS at various different lens aperture/film speed settings, so long as any change in one setting is compensated for by an equal and opposite change in the other. For instance, in the sample table 3 below, each of these combinations of settings would give the same exposure value given, say, an ISO 100 (or equivalent) film/PS rating.

With the advent of digital capture technology in photography, increasingly you are able to compensate for a change in lens aperture or shutter speed by altering the sensitivity of the image capture material. With traditional film cameras, a films ISO rating could be determined only for the entire roll and, once set, could not practically be changed (with the exception of large-format cameras using sheet film). However, digital capture has changed things considerably. Because digital capture allows you to set an ISO equivalency for each individual frame you could, for example, compensate for a one-stop increase in shutter speed by increasing the ISO equivalency rating by one stop, say from 200 to 400. In the sample table 4 shown below, each of the given exposure setting combinations would produce an equal exposure value.

Better than average

Having said all this why not just set the camera to the full (programmed) automatic exposure setting and let it make all the

Table 3 – Lens aperture / shutter speed combinations that produce identical exposure values

Lens aperture	Shutter speed (seconds)	Exposure value (EV)
f/4	1/500	13
f/5.6	1/250	13
f/8	1/125	13
f/11	1/60	13
f/16	1/30	13

Note: Also refer to EV diagram on page 53

Table 4 – Lens aperture / shutter speed / ISO (ISO equivalency) rating combinations that produce identical exposure values

Lens aperture	Shutter speed (seconds)	ISO (ISO equivalency) rating	Exposure value (EV)
f/4	1/250	200	11
f/4	1/125	100	11
f/4	1/500	400	11
f/2.8	1/250	100	11
f/5.6	1/250	400	11

decisions for you? There are two answers to this question. The first is a technical one relating to the limitation of light meters. The second is an artistic one that has to do with the limitations of the camera.

There is no doubt that a lot of time, money and effort has been spent over the past few years by the Research & Development departments of the major camera manufacturers in attempting to develop the ultimate light meter. It is also fair to say that some have come close. Currently, I use Nikon's F5 and D100 cameras in my main arsenal and they both have highly accurate metering systems.

However, as with any system designed to work in diverse conditions, camera light meters have to work either on averages or by recognizing scenes compared with preset precedents. Now, the former is fine if you're photographing a scene in average lighting, with average tones and, therefore, minimal contrast. But you want to make pictures that are better than average and so must learn how to cope with extremes, which is something the camera just can't do on its own.

Digital exposure

As digital capture technology has become more popular I am now regularly asked questions about how it differs from film photography. The first thing to bear in mind is that digital photography is still photography and, in its purest form, whether you capture an image on a photo-sensor or on film is really neither here nor there. After all, many years ago photographers switched from using plate glass to film but that didn't change the basic principles of the photographic art!

The real beauty of digital capture is that you now have far more control over the in-camera image than you ever had with film and for those of you who, like me, prefer to be out in the field rather than in a darkroom or in front of a computer, this development is the real boon of digital technology. One area that has benefited significantly is exposure, and in more ways than one. First of all the latitude of a digital photo-sensor is even greater than negative film, making dealing with high-contrast scenes far simpler than it used to be. One thing to bear in mind, however, is that this latitude, unlike film, is not even and digital sensors tend to retain detail in shadow more than they do in highlights. For this reason, I frequently underexpose from the suggested meter reading by applying – 1/3 stop.

The other major advantage of digital capture is that you can see instantly the result of your decisions and make immediate changes if anything has gone wrong. This ability to shoot; analyze; alter; re-shoot, has made photographic experimentation a far easier task and generally means you get more successful shots 'in the bag'.

With the more sophisticated cameras that have thousands of pre-programmed exposure scenes and values in their microchips, the issue is one of recognition. It's all very well having a look-up table to get the 'correct' exposure from, but how does the camera know whether it is looking up the right precedent. The honest answer is that it cannot know. It often gets it right, but the difficulty from the photographer's point of view is that you can never be sure when it is getting it right or getting it wrong until you see the finished product, and by then it is too late.

Something else the camera can't do is read your mind. Of course, you can let it guess what you're thinking, which is the equivalent of setting it to full automatic, and one time in a hundred it might get it right. But if you want to make consistently good photographs, and be confident that what you see is what you get, then you must learn to tell the camera your thoughts and get it to react as you infer.

Every change to a camera's settings changes the final image. Not only will those changes affect things like depth of field, motion blur and graininess (or noise in the case of digital), they will also affect the mood, emotion and graphic statement contained within the photograph.

Sometimes the changes will be only subtle, and hardly apparent to the uninformed observer at all. But they are what makes your photographs yours – your personal statement – and what makes the difference between a good picture and a compelling one.

◀▼ *Slight changes in lens aperture, shutter speed or ISO rating can massively alter the statement a photograph makes. The first image was shot using aperture priority autoexposure. For the second image I used manual metering and adjusted the shutter speed down, and rated the ISO equivalency up one stop. Although similar, they tell completely different stories.*

Seeing the light

We tend to take light for granted – it's there when we wake up each morning and remains with us throughout the day. We notice when it's gone but how much attention do you really pay it? When you first start learning about photography invariably you read about the 'quality' of light. But what does this really mean in a practical sense? For photographers, light is everything and learning how to see and read light will not only make understanding exposure a far simpler process it will also add greatly to the overall quality of your photographs.

◀ *Evening light breaks through dense storm clouds to create an ethereal vision of the close of day.*

35mm camera, 80mm lens, Fuji Velvia, 1/30sec at f/5.6

Light at work

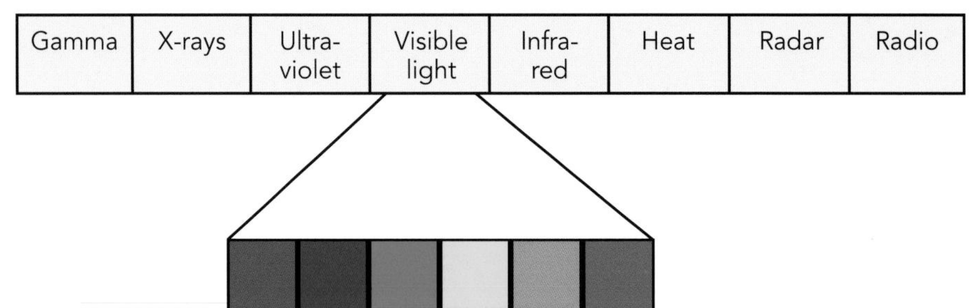

▲ *The above diagram illustrates some of the electromagnetic spectrum and the small part of it that forms visible light. Some of the other wavelengths you will know, such as radio waves and heat, while others you will recognize in photographic terms, such as ultraviolet light and infrared. The principal colours of the visible spectrum – violet, blue, green, yellow, orange and red – are commonly seen in rainbows.*

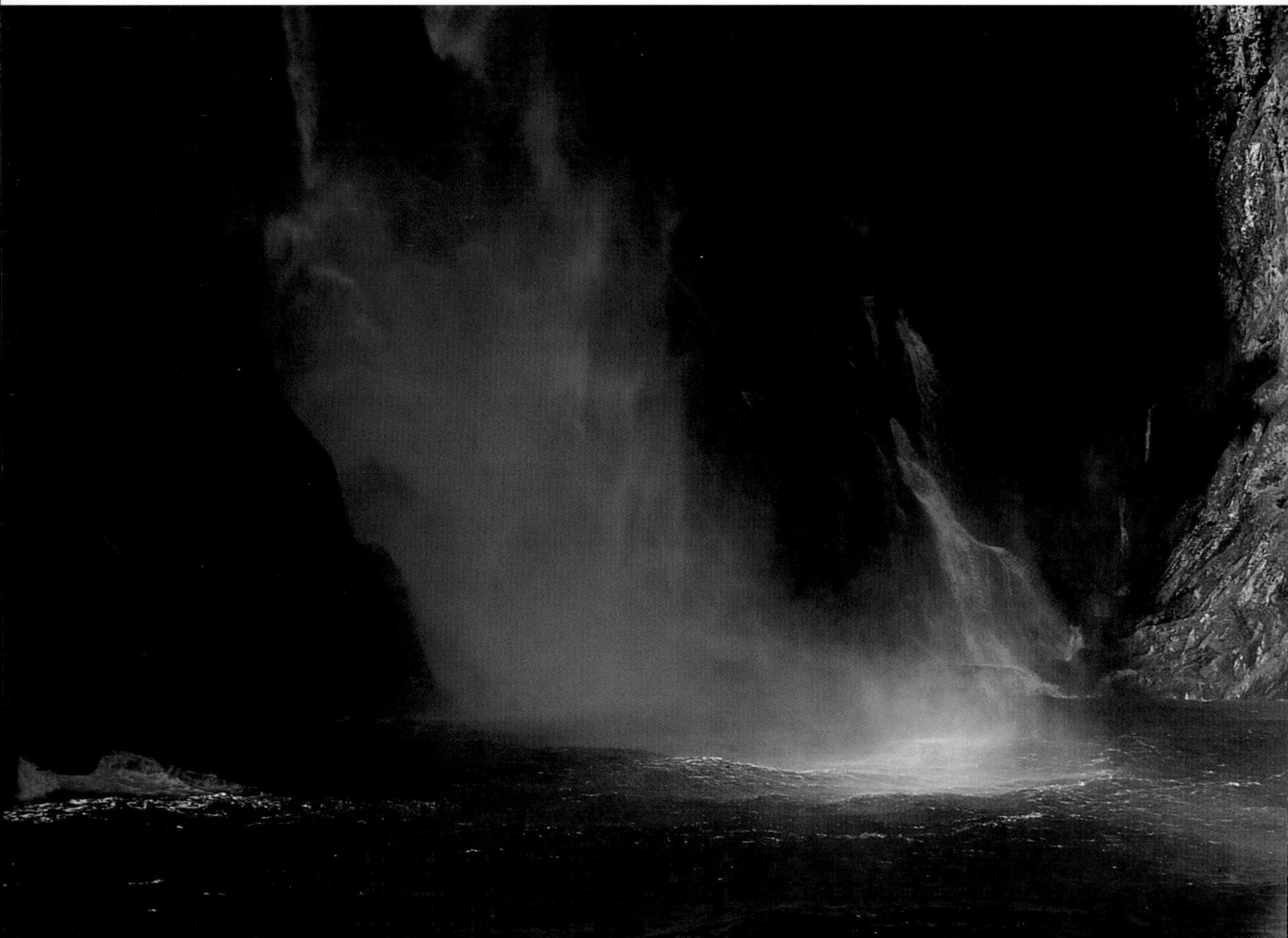

If you studied basic physics at school then you will probably understand the principal characteristics of light. However, for those of you to whom, like me, school seems a long time ago, let me refresh your memory. Human beings, and therefore by default cameras, see light in terms of waves. As far as science is concerned these waves are of multiple length but only a fraction of them are visible to the naked eye. These visible waves are called 'visible light' and, from the photographic perspective, are what we are most interested in. Light waves also have different frequencies and, without getting too bogged down in physics, it is these frequencies that give us another of the key components of the photographic art, colour.

The colour of light

We can decipher many millions of colours but all of them are a combination of some or all of the six principal colours of the visible light spectrum – red, orange, yellow, green, blue and violet. If you were to mix all six in equal proportions you would get white, colourless light.

▼ *The rainbows below, taken at Milford Sound on the South Island of New Zealand, display the whole spectrum of visible colours.*

35mm panoramic camera, 45mm lens, Fuji Provia, 1/60sec at f/8

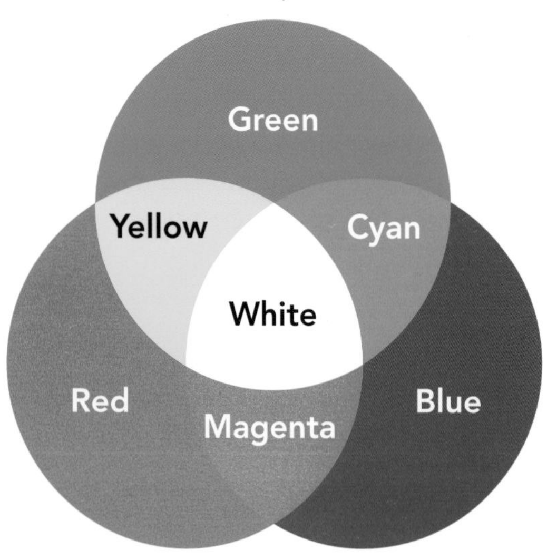

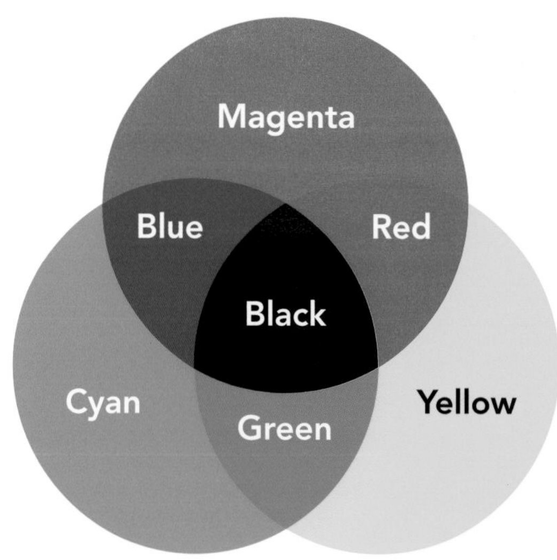

▲ *The colours we see are created either by addition (left) or subtraction (right), as shown in the diagrams above.*

This mixing of colours is apparent in photography. Film, digital photo-sensors and computer monitors all add colours (red, green and blue) to produce colour images. For example, an equal mix of blue and green will produce cyan; red and blue will produce magenta; and green and red will produce yellow. Mixing all three colours equally will give you white. On the other hand ink jet printers and photographic enlargers produce colour by subtraction. Look at the dials on a colour enlarger and you will see cyan, magenta and yellow. By mixing yellow and cyan you get green; cyan and magenta will give you blue; and magenta and yellow gives you red. Combine all three and you get black. Another photographic example of colour by subtraction is colour correction filters. For instance, placing an '81 series' orange filter in front of your lens will absorb some of the blue light that predominates during the middle of the day leaving warm red and neutral green light to produce a much warmer overtone in the resulting image.

Blowing hot and cold

I use the term 'warmer' above because colour is often defined in terms of its relative temperature. Warm colours, such as orange, red and yellow are the colours you see at sunrise, in the early morning and at sunset. People respond positively to warm colours, associating them with positive emotions. Conversely, blue is considered a cool colour and photographs with a high level of blue in them will make you feel chilled, which can be exploited in photographic composition when that is the emotional response you are trying to evoke – in a winter landscape, perhaps.

▲ *Compare these two images and decide which scene you'd prefer to be walking in. People have a natural preference for the warmer colours of the spectrum.*

Table 5 – Colour temperature of light sources

Light source	Temperature (K)
Clear blue sky	10,000–15,000
Shade on sunny day	7,500
Overcast (cloudy) day	6,000–8,000
Noon sunlight	6,500
Average daylight (4 hours before sunset and 4 hours after sunrise)	5,500
Early AM / late PM	4,000
1 hour before sunset	3,500
Sunset	2,500
Electronic flash	5,500
Fluorescent light	4,200
Household lightbulb (100W)	2,900
Studio tungsten light	3,200
Candlelight	2,000

Colour temperature is measured on the Kelvin scale, in degrees kelvin (K) (see table 5), and its relevance to your photography, beyond its compositional properties, is in how film and digital photo-sensors respond to light. The human eye is a very sophisticated tool and, in conjunction with your brain, automatically compensates for differences in colour temperature so that you rarely notice much of a change. Photo-sensitive materials are less capable of such high levels of compensation and will record light as it sees it. Which means, for example, that the blue colour cast apparent, yet invisible to you, during the middle of the day is recorded on film/PSs exactly as that – blue colour. Also, because the manufacturers have to draw a line in the sand, most film and, to some extent, digital photo-sensors are calibrated to read light as average daylight and will record colour temperature based on their pre-defined settings.

What this means is that any light source other than average daylight (fours hours after sunrise and four hours before sunset), which is measured at 5,500K, will be recorded with either a blue colour cast (temperatures above 5,500K) or with an orange colour cast (temperatures below 5,500K).

Sometimes, the effect of this colour cast is pleasing to the eye. For example, it is unlikely that you would want a beautiful golden sunrise or sunset to appear as anything other than just that and so you would probably use no colour correction at all.

However, at other times you may want to add some colour correction. Usually, this is the case when photographing with artificial light using daylight-balanced film or when the colour temperature is much higher than the average 5,500K, which produces images with a strong blue colour cast.

▲ *Sometimes colour casts produce preferable results and compensating for the effects of a golden sunset on daylight-balanced film may produce an effect you'd rather avoid.*

▼▶ *There are times when the 'invisible' colour of light will need to be rectified by using colour correction filters or digital white balance. For example, look closely at the two images of the ostrich.*

◄▼ *Both were taken with a digital camera, the first with WB set to daylight. Changing the setting to 'cloudy' has added a touch of warmth to the picture that greatly enhances its appeal.*

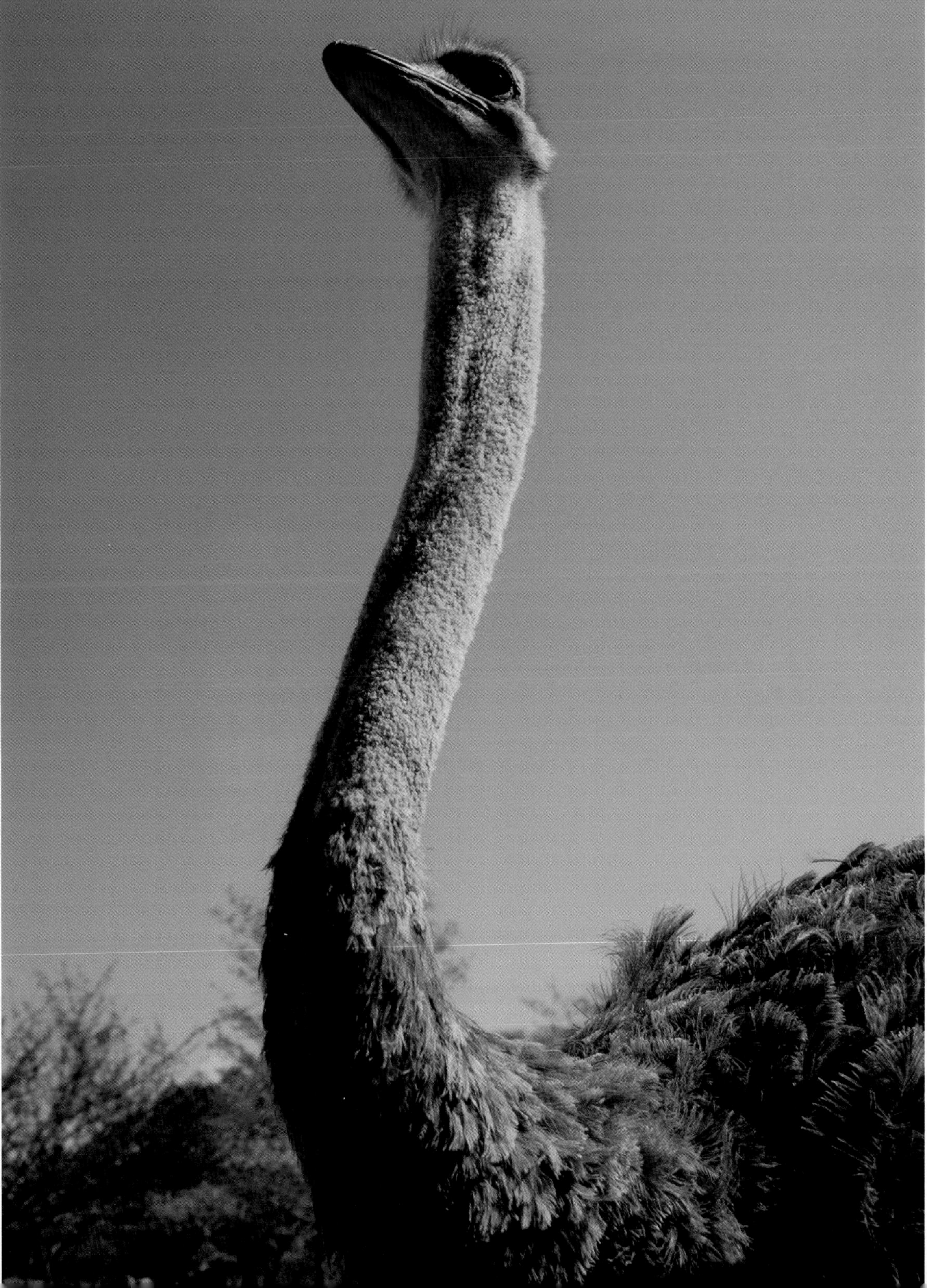

Table 6 – Recommended filters for colour correction

Light source	Colour correction filter (daylight-balanced film)	WB setting (digital)
Clear blue sky	85B	Shade
Shade on sunny day	81C	Shade
Overcast (cloudy) day	81B	Cloudy
Noon sunlight	81B	Cloudy
Average daylight (4 hours before sunset and 4 hours after sunrise)	81A	Cloudy
Early AM / late PM	81A	Cloudy
1 hour before sunset	81A	Cloudy
Sunset	None	Cloudy
Electronic flash	None	Flash
Fluorescent light	82C	Fluorescent
Household lightbulb (100W)	80A + 82C	Incandescent
Studio tungsten light	80A	Incandescent
Candlelight	None	Incandescent

In table 6 above, I have listed some of my own preferences for using colour correction filters, which you are welcome to copy. As always, please remember that they are personal choices and you may want to experiment with your own ideas.

White balance (WB)

The advent of digital capture technology has given a far greater level of control to photographers than is available with film. For example, while film, at the point of manufacture, can be balanced only for a single colour temperature (usually daylight or tungsten light), digital photo-sensors can be balanced for different colour temperatures with each different shot. In this way the ability of a digital PS to compensate for changes in colour temperature is much closer to that of the human eye.

Many digital cameras come with WB settings pre-programmed, the more common of which are listed below, along with their relative colour temperature equivalents. More advanced digital cameras also allow you to match exactly the colour temperature at the point of shooting, which gives you the greatest level of control over all conditions.

▲ Top image: Incandescent
▲ Middle image: Fluorescent
▲ Bottom image: Direct sunlight

▲ Top image: Flash
▲ Middle image: Cloudy
▲ Bottom image: Shade

Table 7 – White Balance preferences

WB setting	Approximate colour temperature	
Incandescent	3,000K	(tungsten lightbulb)
Fluorescent	4,200K	(flourescent tube lighting)
Direct sunlight	5,200K	(a similar setting to daylight-balanced film)
Flash	5,400K	
Cloudy	6,000K	
Shade	8,000K	

As you will see from table 7, when shooting digital I often use a WB setting other than that recommended by the camera. For example, under average daylight conditions I will set the WB to 'cloudy' rather than 'direct sunlight'. This is because, more often than not, my style of photography dictates that my images have a warm colour cast. Again, this is a personal preference and, to some extent a commercially based decision. Whether you follow my lead is a conclusion you must come to based on your own experience and experimentation.

Intensity and contrast

Another important facet of photography, particularly in relation to exposure, is the intensity of light. Light intensity is determined by the size of the light source and its distance from the subject.

Sunlight

In terms of distance, sunlight is fixed. Sure, you can claim that by climbing a mountain you are getting closer to the sun but, in reality, the difference is so infinitesimally small that it really makes no difference at all.

In terms of size, however, sunlight can vary. Direct sunlight (that seen on a cloudless day)

▼▶ *Sunlight can be either a point source, creating hard shadows and contrast (below) or, on overcast days, a large light source, creating a much softer quality of light that reduces contrast and produces less well-defined shadows (right).*

is considered a small, point light source. The reason for this is that although, in physical terms, the sun is very big its vast distance from the earth reduces its size relative to objects on the earth's surface. On an overcast day, when the direct rays of the sun are scattered into many new straight lines of light by the cloud cover, the sun becomes a large light source, which produces a very different quality of light – more on that later.

Artificial light

With artificial light you get to play God, with complete control over both the size of the light source and its distance from the subject, and any changes you make can have a distinct effect on the intensity of light falling on your subject. For example, while moving a few steps closer to a waterfall will make very little difference to your exposure settings, moving a studio light the same distance closer to your subject will change your exposure drastically. Distance will also determine the size of the light source in studio photography. A small, point light source, such as a studio reflector, for example, can become a large light source when placed very close to a small subject. Putting a diffuser, such as a soft box, over a point light source will also change the size of the light source, in the same way that cloud cover changes the relative size of light from the sun. Doing so will also change your exposure settings, even if the light to subject distance remains unaltered.

▼ *Like sunlight, artificial light can be either hard or soft in quality. Compare these two images and notice how the soft lighting used in the first picture creates a much gentler image than the hard lighting used in the second picture.*

Contrast

One key factor of photography that is influenced by the intensity of light is contrast. Contrast is the measure of the difference between the highlights and shadows in a given scene. Once again, this is an area where our own eyes are our worst enemy. Humans are capable of seeing detail in both highlights and shadows with a high degree of latitude. Film and digital photo-sensors, however, have limited latitude and so, when calculating exposures you must learn to see like the medium you're using to record the image. Contrast is greater under direct lighting conditions, such as those created by point light sources (such as the sun) and when that source is directly to the side or above the subject. Under diffused conditions, and when the source is in front of the subject, the level of contrast is reduced.

▼ *Contrast, while sometimes being difficult to work with, gives your images three-dimensional form by emphasizing contours. Look at these two pictures and study how the direction of the light has changed the appearance of the model. In the first image, the lighting has produced a very flat picture with very little contrast. In the second image, however, the lighting has been changed to create shadows on one side of the models face, which helps to accentuate her form.*

Quality

Something else you will notice, depending on the lighting conditions, is the quality of the light. Point light sources produce shadows that are harsh and well defined and are described as having a 'hard' quality. Diffused light sources, on the other hand, produce shadows that are much softer with less well-defined edges and are referred to as having a 'soft' quality. The quality of light greatly affects the way your subjects appear in photographs and, while there are always exceptions to the rule, certain subjects are reproduced better under complimentary and sympathetic conditions. For example, portraits of people rarely look pleasing in hard light conditions, while landscape photographers often prefer well-defined shadows that can create very evocative images.

Coming at you from all angles

The final element I'm going to consider in this chapter is the direction of light. Once again, this is a key element to how your subject appears in the final image. Photographs are two-dimensional and yet the world around us is three-dimensional. How, then, do you cross the chasm between the two? The answer is in using the direction of light to create the effects you want. Typically, light comes from one of four places: the side, above, in front and behind.

Front lighting

You are probably all too familiar with the old saying, 'Always photograph with the sun behind you.' Such advice was coined when photography first became fashionable and open to everyone, (rather than just scientists) and had more to do with the limitations of consumer cameras like the Kodak Box Brownie then it had to do with good photography. Lighting a subject from the front will produce acceptable images but often those images will appear very flat and lacking in form. Front lighting also reduces contrast, which can remove the appearance of texture, although this same disadvantage becomes advantageous when you are simply trying to record subjects' key features.

▼ *Front lighting tends to produce flat images that lack contrast and depth.*

Lighting from above

Overhead lighting is typical of the light you'll encounter in the middle of the day and is avoided by most photographers, particularly if that light is of a 'hard' quality. However, there are occasions when you can turn light from above to your advantage. If, for example, your subject has texture that is horizontally formed then direct lighting from above will produce small shadows below each undulation that will help to emphasize form.

▼ *Lighting from above can accentuate linear texture, by creating shadows below each undulation.*

Side lighting

If you are trying to create the appearance of a three-dimensional image then side lighting is going to be your preferred option. Lighting that falls on a subject from the side creates shadows that punctuate texture and define the sides of multi-dimensional objects, such as buildings. It is these shadows that give form to your photographs and help to turn them from flat pieces of paper into pictures with high visual energy.

▼ *Side lighting is the best form of lighting for creating three-dimensional images that highlight form as well as texture.*

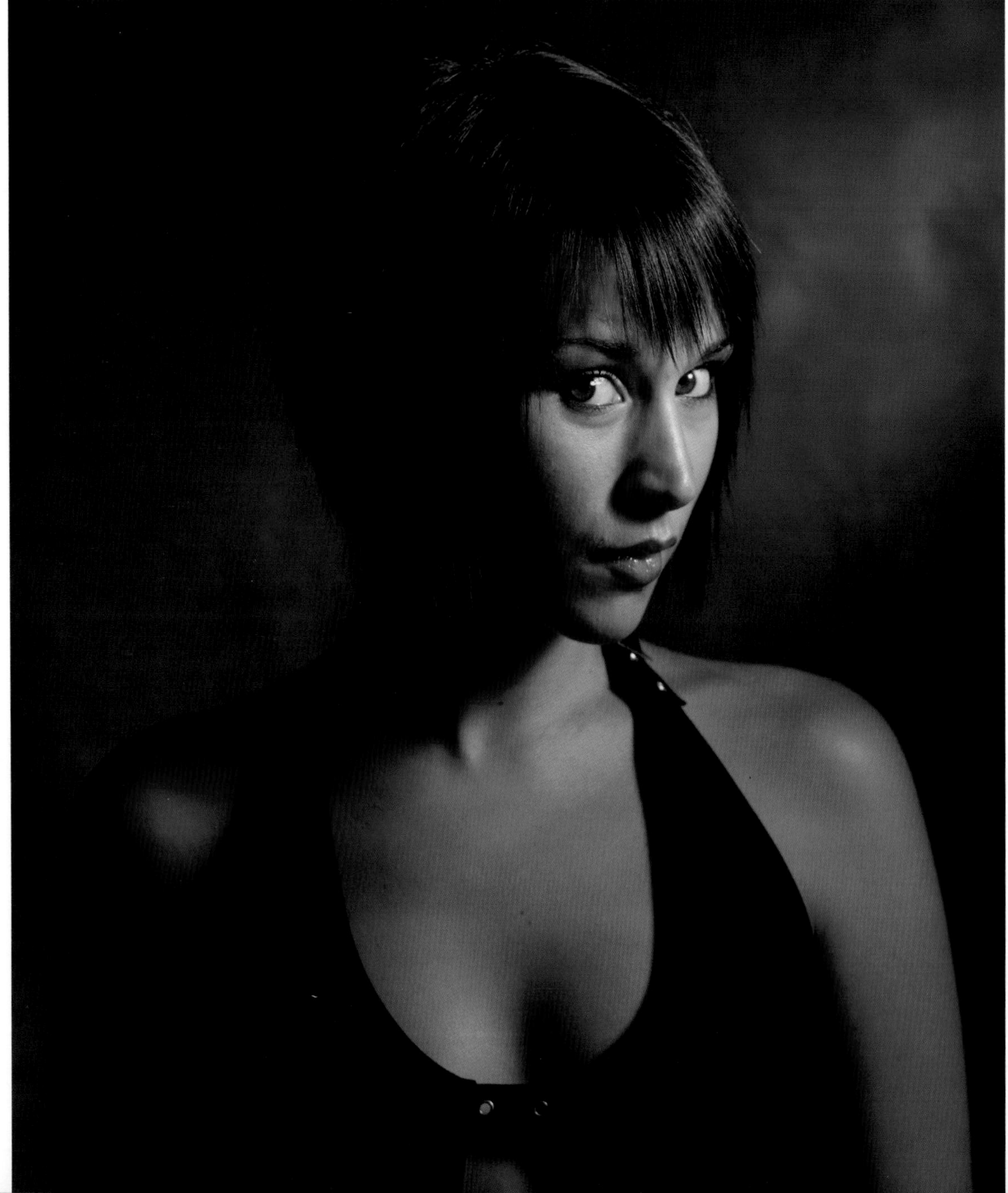

Backlighting

Once again, ignoring the age-old advice never to shoot into the sun can produce some of the classic compositions in photography, such as silhouettes and the 'golden halo' of rim light around a subject. Getting this effect right often depends on your ability to get the exposure right, which, thinking about it, is the perfect lead in to the rest of the book.

▼ *Backlighting can help create powerful photographic compositions such as silhouettes.*

Chapter 3

Tools of the trade

Now that the basics are covered and before I go on to look at the practice of exposure control, it is worth spending some time looking at the tools available to help you in your quest for faithful exposures. Most of you will be familiar with the standard issue through-the-lens (TTL) meter fitted to most modern single lens reflex cameras (SLRs). What may be less obvious is how exactly these meters work, some of the alternative options open to you and when is the right time to employ which tool.

◀ *A correct exposure has kept the detail in these upturned boat-buildings on Lindisfarne, Northumberland, England.*

35mm camera, 24mm lens, Fuji Velvia, 1/50sec at f/16

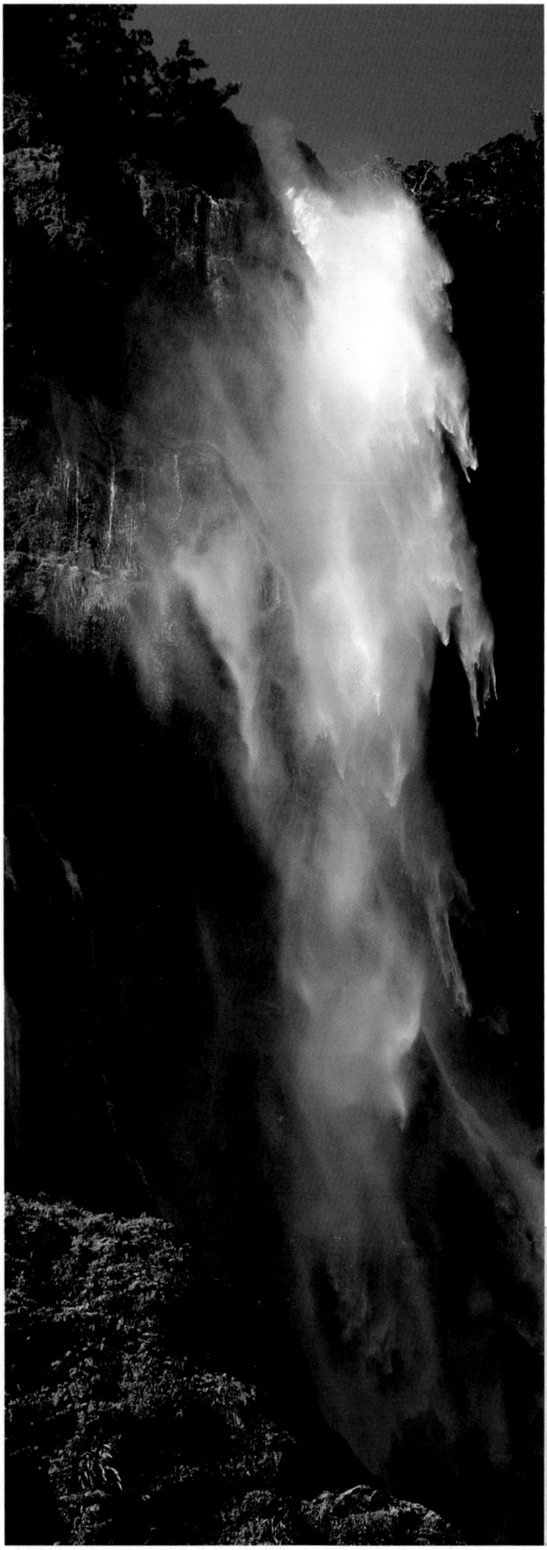

Reflected light meters

When we look at a subject, other than directly at the light source itself, what we see, and therefore what the camera sees also, is reflected light. This light is measured with a reflected light meter (also known as a luminance meter). We perceive a subject's visual brightness based on the amount of reflected light and a reflected light meter converts the perceived brightness of the subject into values that can be interpreted by the photographer to calculate exposure settings. This may be in the form of an exposure value (EV) or in the form of an actual lens aperture/shutter speed combination, depending on the meter used.

One of the principle advantages of the reflected light meter is its practicality. Because you are measuring reflected light you don't need to be in the direct vicinity of the subject – a definite advantage if, like me, you photograph large predatory animals. This also means that the light meter can be built into the camera and this is where we get through-the-lens (TTL) metering.

The main disadvantage of the reflected light meter is in the way it 'sees' variations in tone. Reflected light meters are calibrated to 'see' everything as an average, or middle tone – often known as 18% grey – even when it isn't.

◀ *Using the right light meter in the right way is essential for calculating faithful exposures of scenes such as this one, taken at Stirling Falls, South Island, New Zealand.*

35mm panoramic camera, 45mm lens, Fuji Velvia, 1/200sec at f/8

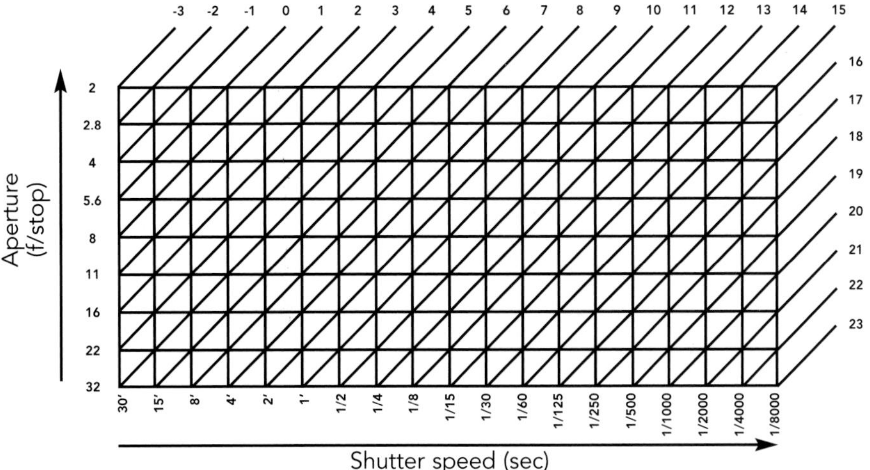

▲ *Some meters give an exposure calculation as an EV number. This number can be referred to the diagram (above) to determine the correct combination of camera settings. For example, an EV of 8 would be the equivalent of 1/60sec at f/2, 1/30sec at f/2.8, 1/15sec at f/4, and so on.*

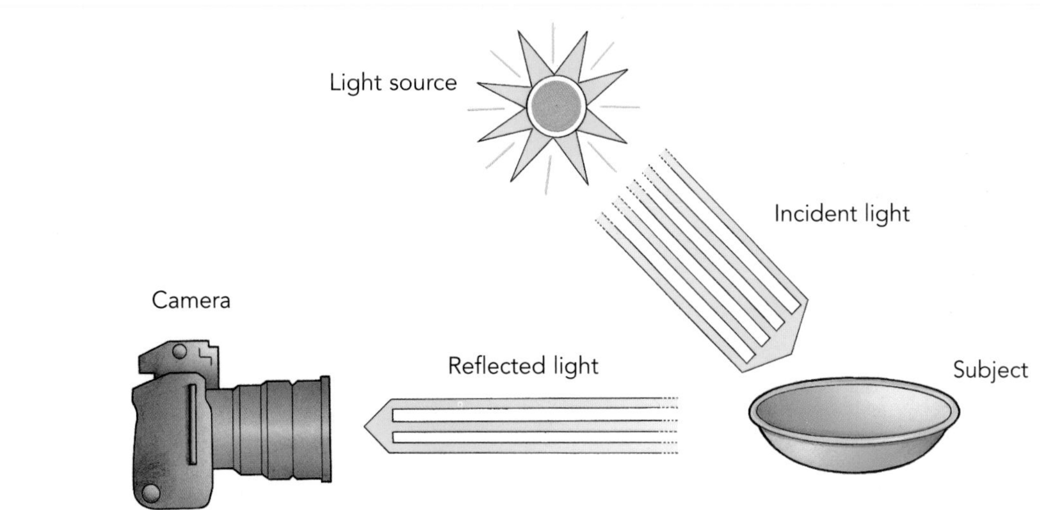

▲ *Reflected light meters, such as in-built TTL meters, read the light reflecting off a subject. They are the most practical form of photographic light meter and, arguably, the most accurate.*

But different coloured subjects reflect different amounts of the light falling on them, (e.g. a yellow daffodil flower will reflect more light than a dark green conifer tree). What this means in practice is that the meter will assume that the subject is reflecting 18% of the light falling on it and will give a reading based on that assumption. However, any subject that is lighter or darker than mid-tone, such as white or black, will reflect more or less light, respectively. The reflected light meter will then be fooled into providing a technically inaccurate reading and, in this example, whites and blacks will come out grey in the final image. For more on this subject, see page 84.

This white bench was first photographed with the camera set to autoexposure and is underexposed. Left to its own devices the light meter has rendered the subject as mid-tone grey. By adding two stops compensation, for the second image, a more natural result has been achieved.

◄ *1/60sec at f/8 – ISO 50*
▼ *1/30sec at f/5.6 – ISO 50*

Similarly, this picture taken on Lindisfarne, Northumberland, shows the black building being rendered grey by the autoexposure meter. Reducing the exposure by two stops has darkened the image, giving a more realistic representation of the scene.

◀ *1/60sec at f/16 – ISO 50*
▼ *1/2000sec at f/16 – ISO 50*

Reflected light meters

Advantages

Negate the need to be close to the subject

Allows complete control over exposure calculations

Can be built into the camera

Disadvantages

Wide measuring angles can distort the light reading

Can be fooled by variations in light and dark tones

TTL meters

Most modern 35mm and digital SLR cameras come with a built-in TTL meter that measures the light actually entering the lens. TTL meters are reflected light meters, with all the attributes – good and bad – noted previously. However, they do hold a couple of advantages over their hand-held cousins. Firstly, because they come with the camera they negate the need to carry an additional accessory. Also, because they are measuring the actual light entering the lens, they automatically take account of external factors, such as any filters in use or the high magnification of macro lenses. On the other hand, they tend to be less selective than a hand-held meter and therefore can suffer more from the distortions caused by wide measuring angles. For example, the area of measurement of a hand-held spot meter is usually around 1°, while that of even the best TTL meters are closer to 3°–5°.

▼ *The advantage of a TTL light meter is that it measures the light actually entering the lens and, therefore, takes into account all accessories placed in front of the lens or between the lens and the camera, such as filters and close-up extension tubes.*

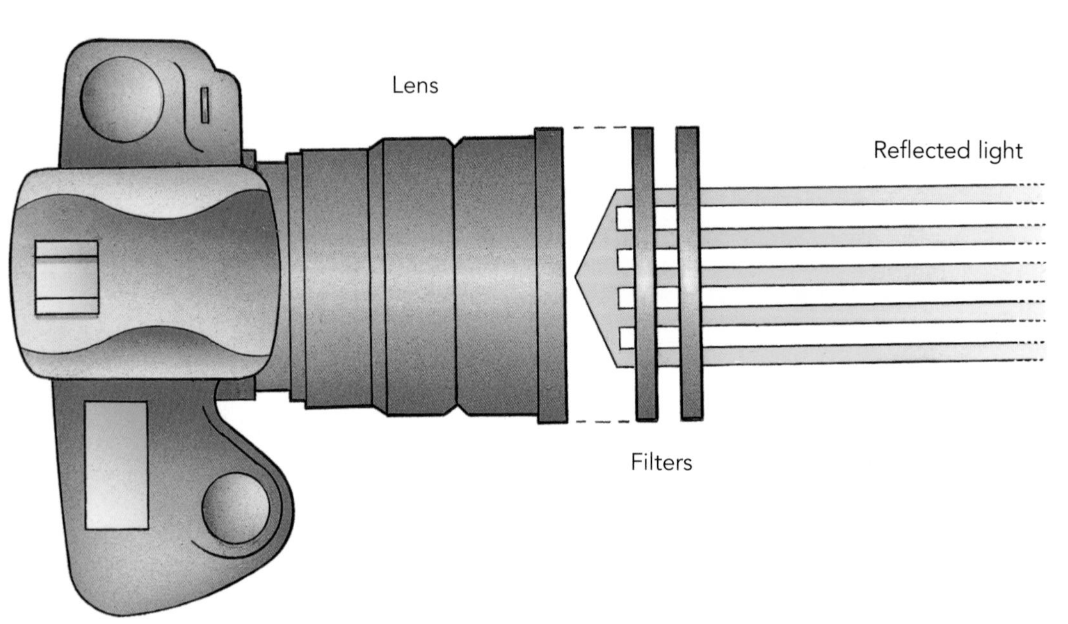

TTL light meters

Advantages

Take into account external factors, such as filters attached and high magnification

Are built into the camera

Often come with multiple-function exposure systems

Disadvantages

Don't always provide the degree of accuracy of a hand-held meter

Sometimes requires re-framing of the composition

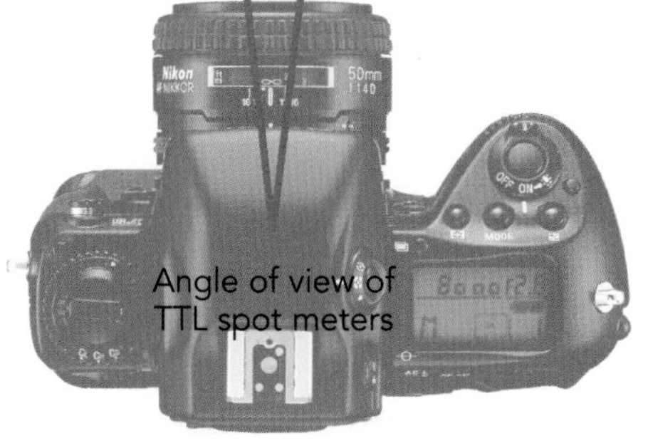

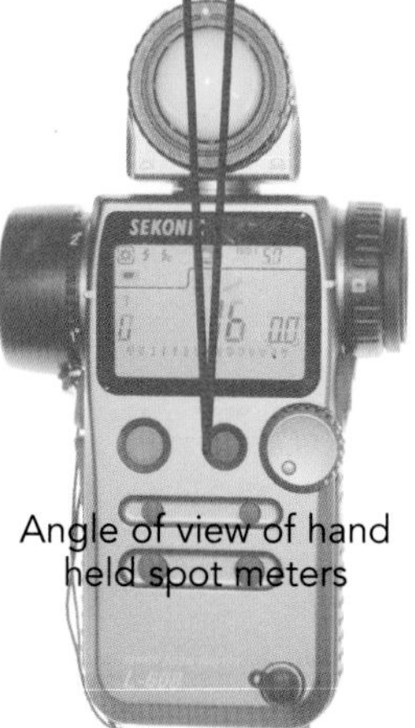

Angle of view of hand
held spot meters

▲ *Spot meters built in to the camera generally have a field of vision of between 3° and 5°. Hand-held meters, on the other hand, have an even narrower field of view, often as little as 1° , which makes them more accurate for complex lighting situations.*

Multiple-function exposure systems

When TTL metering was first introduced it was quite basic compared to more modern systems. Most TTL meters today can be operated with one of three different types of exposure system:

1. multi-segment,
2. centre-weighted, and
3. spot metering.

Multi-segment metering

As its name suggests, a multi-segment metering system takes several independent readings from different areas of the scene and calculates a meter reading based on the findings. Some systems are more sophisticated than others, such as the system built into the Nikon F5, which also uses camera-to-subject distance information and subject colour in the final equation.

This type of metering system is often the most accurate when photographing a scene where the level of contrast falls within the latitude range of the film/PS used and where there is an even distribution of middle tones.

Centre-weighted metering

With centre-weighted metering the TTL meter reads the light across the whole scene but weights the light reading towards the centre portion. Usually around 75% of the reading is based on a centre circle around 12mm in diameter, as seen through the viewfinder. This is ideal for portrait photography, where the subject stands out from the background and fills a large portion of the image space.

Spot metering

When set to spot metering mode, the TTL meter takes a reading from a very small part of the scene – usually an area no more than 3°–5° of the whole. This allows for very precise

▼ *Multi-segment TTL meters take data from many areas of the viewfinder and calculate an exposure value based on the findings, sometimes in relation to a database of actual images stored in the camera's memory banks.*

▼ *Centre-weighted metering systems as they weight the majority of the exposure calculation in the centre circle of the viewfinder. This is useful if the subject fills the centre of the frame. It also takes into account some of the surrounding scene.*

metering of specific areas and provides the greatest level of creative control over your exposure settings. It is particularly useful when dealing with high-contrast scenes and scenes where the intensity of light is diverse.

▼ *Spot meters provide by far the greatest level of flexibility of any metering system. They can read light levels from very small areas of a scene, giving you complete artistic control over the final image.*

Hand-held reflective light meters

If your camera has a built-in TTL meter you could be forgiven for asking why you would want a hand-held meter as well. If your camera doesn't have a built-in meter you are probably in a good position to answer that question for me.

Hand-held reflected light meters are the most versatile meters available. Many have been the occasions that I've been thankful for my hand-held meter when, with my camera mounted on a tripod and my composition set just so, the light has changed necessitating a new meter reading. With a hand-held meter there is no need to change the camera position, you simply take a new reading independently of

▼ *A hand-held reflective light meter can be a useful accessory to carry, even if your camera has a built-in light meter.*

the camera and make any necessary adjustments without disturbing your composition.

The best hand-held reflected light meters offer a 1° spot metering facility, which allows you to assess the brightness of very specific parts of the overall scene, from which to calculate your exposure values. This makes them far more accurate than even the best TTL meters in spot mode and provides you with ultimate exposure control in any conditions.

On the downside it is an additional accessory for you to carry (which may be an issue if you are needing to travel light) and they do not automatically take into account any external factors such as any filtration you may be using. This can be particularly apparent when using polarizing filters, where the degree of exposure compensation is less easily calculated than a fixed filter, such as an 81 series.

Hand-held reflected light meters

Advantages

Extremely versatile and independent of the camera

Narrow field of measurement giving greater accuracy

Complete creative control

Disadvantages

Additional accessory to carry

Don't take into account external factors, such as filters used or magnification

Most hand-held meters only offer a single metering mode for reflected light.

Incident light meters

Rather than measuring the light reflecting from a subject, it is possible to measure the amount of light falling on a subject. This is referred to as incident light or illumination and can be measured with a hand-held incident light meter.

An incident light meter has a white plastic dome, or invercone, which averages the total amount of light falling on it before the diffused level of light is measured by the meter's cell. For best results an incident light meter should ideally be placed close to the subject, pointing

▲ *Incident light meters work in a different way to reflected light meters, measuring the amount of light falling on a subject. They are often used by wedding and portrait photographers and are less vulnerable to high-contrast lighting conditions.*

towards the camera. (Anyone who has witnessed a wedding photographer at work will have seen this in action.) The advantage of this type of metering is that it isn't influenced by contrasting areas of light and dark, as a reflective meter is, and therefore it gives accurate results in most lighting conditions. However, incident meters don't give any selective information, removing a degree of creative control over any potential image.

▼ *Incident light meters measure the level of light falling on a subject, not light reflected. They still give a meter reading based on a mid-tone subject. They are best suited to situations where they can be placed close to the subject being metered.*

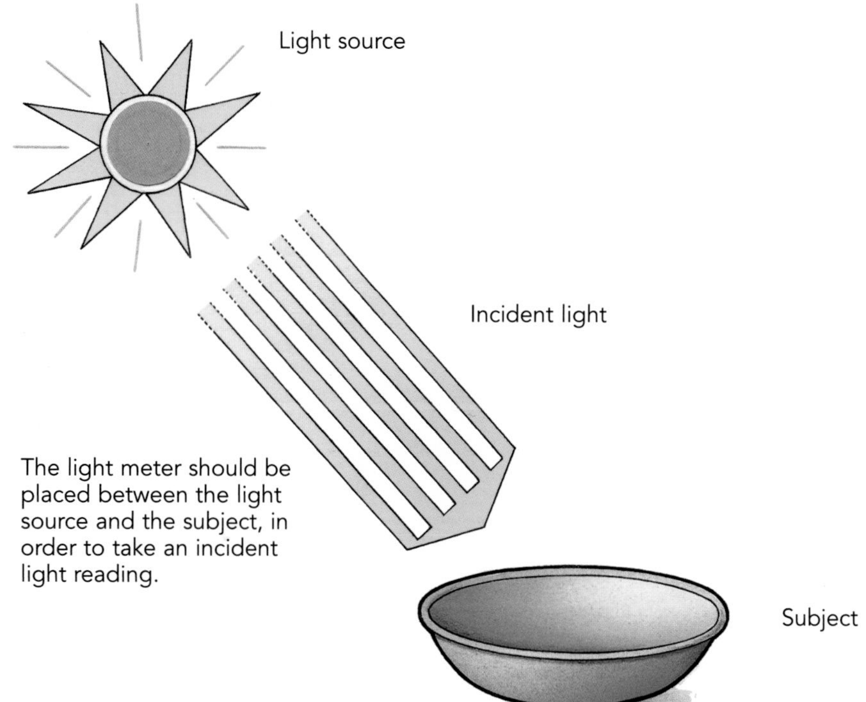
Light source
Incident light
The light meter should be placed between the light source and the subject, in order to take an incident light reading.
Subject

Hand-held incident light meters

Advantages	**Disadvantages**
Not influenced by contrasting light and dark areas in a scene	Needs to be positioned close to the subject for best results
Measures light falling on a subject rather than reflecting off it	Lack of selective information

Other useful stuff to carry

The light meter is the essential tool for calculating exposure values. But there are a couple of other useful items that you should consider keeping with you.

18% grey card

As I have already described, most light meters are calibrated to give a technically accurate meter reading from a subject with a reflectance value of somewhere in the region of 18% – otherwise known as a mid-tone subject. If you are photographing a scene with a reflected light meter where no mid-tone subjects are apparent then metering from an 18% grey card, positioned in the same light as your subject, will give you your technically accurate exposure value for the scene.

These cards can be bought from most good camera stores and are a useful accessory to keep handy. In reality, however, it is often impossible to use. For example, I haven't yet tried asking a grizzly bear if it would mind holding my grey card while I take a meter reading, but I can imagine the kind of response I'd get if I did! Similarly, with distant subjects such as landscapes, at best a grey card will give you an approximation but it is unlikely you'll be able to position it in an appropriate place where the intensity of light is the same for the subject as it is for the card. They are very useful, though, if you can get close to your subject and where the level of light throughout the scene is consistent.

18% Grey Card

▲ *Grey cards can be bought from most photographic retailers and are a handy tool. They work by being placed in the same light as your subject and a meter reading being taken from their surface. Because they are mid-tone, the resulting meter reading should be accurate.*

Your hand

An alternative to using an 18% grey card is to improvise with your own hand. The palm of the hand is approximately one stop brighter than mid-tone. If you take a meter reading of your palm and increase the exposure value by one stop you will have obtained the same result as if you had used an 18% grey card.

Getting the most from your tools

Calibrating your meter

Earlier on I told you that all light meters are calibrated to read light assuming a reflectance value of 18% – mid-tone. Well, they are – and they aren't. Although there is an international standard governing calibration a little latitude always applies and different light meters will give contrary readings when measuring the same light.

To ensure absolute technical accuracy in the measurements given by your own light meter it is recommended that you run a calibration test of your own. To calibrate your meter follow the steps outlined below using a grey card (described on page 62).

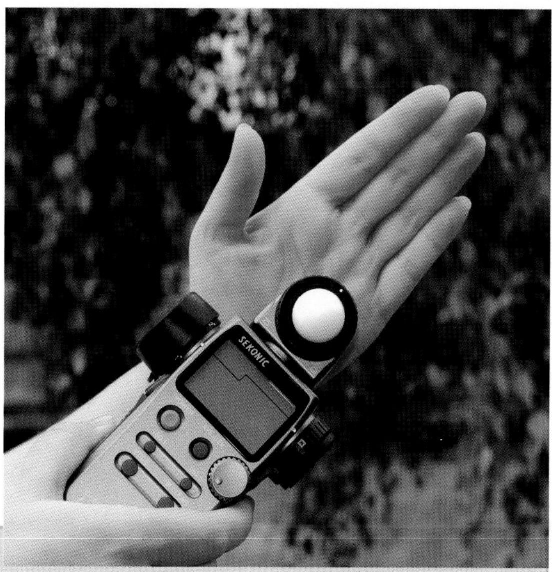

◄▲ *If you don't have a grey card or have forgotten to take it with you then the palm of your hand can be used. The palm of the hand is one stop brighter than mid-tone.*

1. Place the card in flat, consistent light conditions. An overcast day is ideal.
2. Using a tripod, if possible, position your camera with a standard lens attached so that the image of the card fills the viewfinder. Ensure the card is in focus.
3. Set the camera to DX coding or manually set the film speed to the manufacturer's ISO rating. (If using a digital camera set the camera to a commonly used ISO equivalency rating, e.g. 200.) Select manual exposure mode on the camera.
4. Set the exposure settings on the camera to match the reading given by your meter and take a photograph. This is your base exposure.
5. Keeping the camera in position take eight more pictures at the following settings: Meter reading +2 stops; +1½; +1; +1/2; –1/2; –1; –1½; –2
6. If using film then get the images processed. If you are using a digital camera you will be able to review the results immediately on a computer screen.*
7. Line up the images in order and review them against your grey card. The image that is closest in colour will give you the required compensation setting for your exposures when metering with the tested light meter. If your meter is correctly calibrated from the factory this should be +/–0.

***Note**

Your computer screen must also be calibrated to show an accurate rendition of your digital images.

There is one problem with this procedure, however, when using film because all film is subject to similar fluctuations in latitude during manufacture. Therefore, to be absolutely precise in your calibration test you need to repeat the process with every new batch of film you purchase. And, unless you purchase 'professional' film, this means with every film you purchase. For that reason the calibration test is an often-neglected discipline.

Film

Because all exposure calculations are based around the sensitivity of the film you are using (I'll cover digital in a moment or two), it is worth saying some words about film and the role film plays in exposure control.

Film speed

The sensitivity of a film, that is, how quickly it reacts to light is referred to as the film's speed and is indicated by its ISO rating. Film speeds fall into three categories: fast (ISO 400 and above), medium (ISO 100–200), and slow (ISO 25–64). ISO refers to an industry standard against which all film speed is measured.

The faster the film the more quickly it reacts to light. Typically, photographers use fast films when gaining additional stops of light is important. For example, when photographing wildlife I often have to shoot at dawn and twilight when the animals are more active. But, if I'm trying to freeze motion I still need to use a fast shutter speed. Without fast film, even with the lens set to maximum aperture, this is sometimes impossible to achieve.

The faster the film, however, the more grain becomes apparent in the resulting image. Sometimes, grain can produce very atmospheric images, which may be the effect you are trying to achieve. Other times, grain

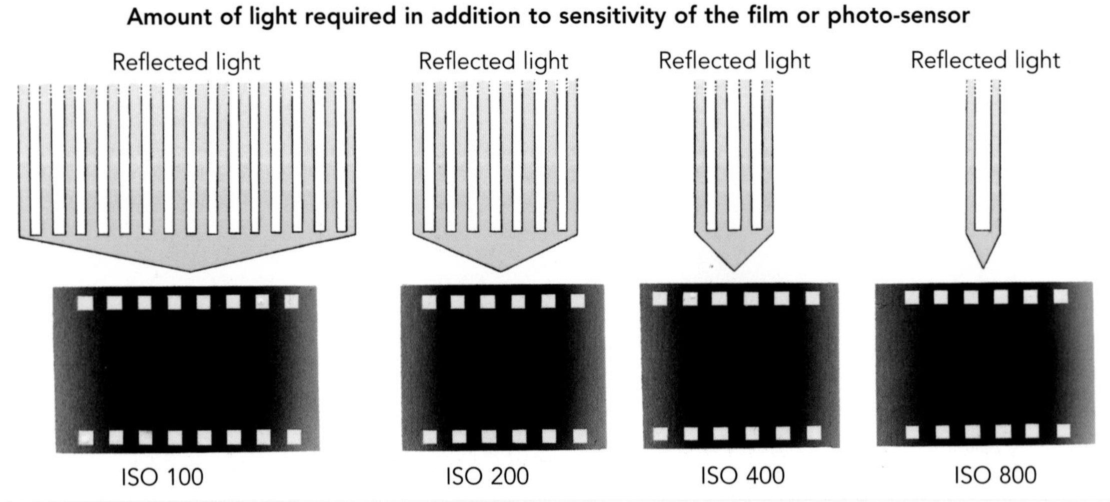

▲ *Film speed is related to the amount of light required for the photosensitive material to react to light. The slower the film the greater the amount of light needed for an image to form.*

can detract from the quality of the image and slower films are a better choice. Certainly for publication purposes, most picture editors look for images that are devoid of grain, which is the reason Fuji Velvia 50 and, previous to the advent of Velvia 50, Kodak's Kodachrome 64 are and were the preferred choice of professional photographers.

▼ *The downside to using fast film is that grain, the size of the crystals used in the film, gets bigger and is more apparent in your photographs. While this can sometimes be used for creative effect is usually best avoided. In digital photography, the same issue arises with digital noise. You can see the progression from a (grainless) to d (grainiest), below.*

Film contrast range

Unlike the human eye, which can detect detail with very broad latitude, film can record detail with very limited latitude. A typical negative film, for example, has a contrast range of seven stops (sometimes depicted as a ratio of 128:1). This means that a negative film can record detail in tones from near featureless black to almost pure white. Slide film, on the other hand, is less forgiving and will record detail within a range of only five stops (ratio 32:1).

The film contrast range becomes relevant when you are photographing a scene with many different tones. Any tones that fall outside of the contrast range of the film you are using will lose all detail and appear as black shadows or washed-out highlights.

▼ *All photosensitive materials have a latitude (the degree to which they show detail in shadows and highlights). None are as good as the human eye and so you must learn to see as the camera sees.*

Tones falling outside the film contrast range.

It is important that you test the contrast range of the films you are using in order to improve the quality and faithfulness of your exposures. To measure the contrast range of a film copy the following steps:

1. Place a medium-toned, flat but textured subject in even, consistent lighting.
2. With the exposure mode set to manual, meter the subject and expose one frame. This will give you your base measurement.
3. Make a series of ten exposures, reducing the exposure setting by 1/2 stop on each occasion.
4. Then, make an additional series of ten exposures, this time increasing the exposure setting by 1/2 stop on each occasion.
5. You will end up with 21 exposed frames. Examine each frame for detail, using the first frame as your starting point. Count the number of frames either side of your base frame in which you can see any detail. The result will be the contrast range of your film.

Film colour response

Different films respond to colours in different ways depending on the balance between the red, green and blue layers that form the emulsion. An equal balance will produce a natural colour response. That is, the subject will appear much the same on film as it is does to the human eye. Some films are purposefully balanced towards a particular colour, however. Therefore, to be able to pre-visualize how the colours in a particular scene will appear on film it is worth testing the film for colour response. Copy the following steps:

1. Acquire a set of similar objects of different colours ensuring they include the colours red, green and blue. (A set of children's building blocks is ideal.)
2. Place them on an even surface under flat, consistent lighting. Include a grey card for reference.
3. Metering from the grey card make an exposure.
4. Examine the results to see how the film responds to the colours.
5. To see how the film responds to colours at different levels of brightness repeat the above process at different exposure settings.

Photo-sensors

Digital cameras use photo-sensors as the light-sensitive material in place of film. In many ways digital capture is a far more flexible medium than film allowing you to alter the ISO equivalency, the contrast range and colour response for individual frames – no longer do you need to carry different film types for different occasions, you simply make the adjustments as you shoot.

It is still important, however, that you test your PS at its standard settings in order to give you a set of base values for noise (equivalent to grain in film), contrast range and colour response. To measure each of these areas simply repeat the tests detailed above for film.

Calculating exposure in six simple steps

Already you will have noticed that achieving faithful exposures takes more than pointing your light meter – in-camera or hand-held – at a scene and accepting what it tells you as the truth, the whole truth and nothing but...

◀ *Exposing for the light in this kind of scene can be a real nightmare. Get it right, however, and you'll be repaid with images like this.*

35mm camera, 24mm lens, Fuji Velvia, 1/250sec at f/22

In the previous two chapters I have touched on the limitations of the light meter and remarked on how your choice of film, lens aperture and shutter speed selection, ISO (and ISO equivalency) rating and personal vision directly affect the appearance of the photographs you make. Getting to grips with these elementary principles of exposure is central to gaining an appreciation of the exposure equation and your ability to make informed decisions when selecting exposure values.

Over the following two chapters I am going to explore in greater detail the process of calculating exposure values, compensating for the limitations of the light meter, applying your creative interpretation and managing extreme conditions.

Setting film speed / ISO equivalency

The first step in the process of calculating exposure is setting your desired film speed or ISO equivalency (in digital capture). If you are using a 35mm or roll film camera then you are limited to setting an ISO rating for the entire film. You are also going to be somewhat tied to the ISO rating of the film in use. However, it is possible to change the nominal ISO rating of the film in use by altering the ISO setting on the camera – if your camera allows manual adjustment and doesn't just work on DX coding. This process is known as up-rating (pushing) or down-rating (pulling) film.

When you up-rate (push) a film you are effectively asking the camera to act as if the film was more sensitive to light, and,

effectively, it becomes a faster film. You may, for example, change the rating of an ISO 100 film to ISO 200 by setting the camera's film speed setting to ISO 200. When the camera's meter takes a reading it will assume this revised rating and give an exposure value accordingly. The purpose behind pushing film is to gain additional stops of light when conditions or circumstances dictate.

Some films react better to being pushed than others and it is never wise to push a film beyond two stops. Before pushing film it is recommended that you refer to the manufacturer's technical guide.

When conditions are very bright you may decide to down-rate (pull) the film, decreasing its nominal ISO rating. The process for pulling film is opposite that of pushing it.

Pushing film is a far more common practice than pulling it. In either case it is important that you tell the processing house what you've done so they process the film accordingly.

Push processing

If you find yourself needing extra speed then rather than switching to a faster film you can rate a slower film at a higher ISO rating. This process is referred to as 'pushing' or 'up-rating' film, and effectively gives you an additional one or two stops of light to work with. (Pushing by more than two stops is not really recommended.) There are a number of reasons you may want to push a film but usually it is because light levels are too low to achieve the desired combination of lens aperture/shutter speed for the exposure you want. Also, some films react particularly well to 'up-rating', so much so that that an ISO 100 film rated at 200 can give better results than a true ISO 200 film. Of course you can only apply this technique to the entire roll of film and it's essential that you tell the processing lab what you've done, otherwise you'll end up with a set of underexposed pictures.

◀ *Low-light photography is an example of where you may want to push film in order to gain additional stops of light. Here I up-rated Fuji Velvia from its factory rating of ISO 50 to ISO 100.*

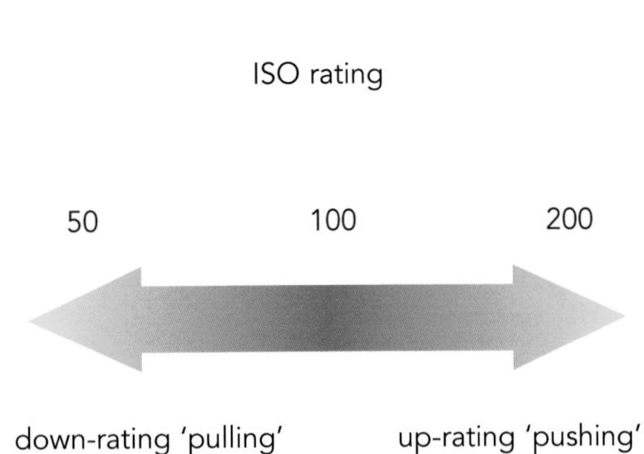

▲ *Film can either be pushed (up-rated) to overexpose or pulled (down-rated) to underexpose. This is compensated for at the processing stage.*

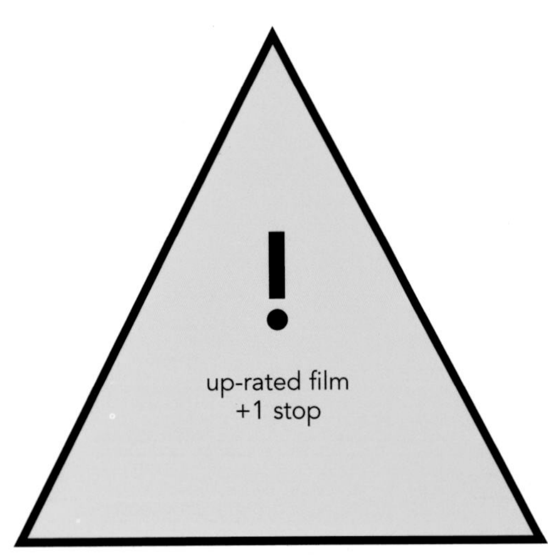

▲ *Mark any up-rated or down-rated film cannister with an appropriate label so that the processor knows what you've done and will compensate.*

Digital capture has made changing the sensitivity of the recording material far more flexible and it is now possible, with some digital cameras, to change the ISO equivalency rating for every shot. As with film, however, remember that the faster the ISO equivalency you set the more 'noise' will appear in the final image.

Deciding the area of the scene to meter from

Because all light meters give an exposure value based on a mid-tone you should first look for an area of the scene that is mid-toned and in the same light as the main subject, from which you can take a base reading. Assuming all other tones in the scene are within the contrast range of the film/PS then they will all appear in the final image as they do to the naked eye.

If no appropriate mid-toned areas exist within the scene then decide on which area of the scene is the primary subject and meter from that subject. Then apply the appropriate exposure compensation factor, as described below.

Taking a meter reading

You would think that this was the easy part, simply point the meter at your subject and 'hey presto', you've got your meter reading. Unfortunately, it's a little more involved than that. How you obtain your meter reading to give a technically accurate result depends on many things, including the type of meter you're using, the exposure mode used by that meter, the subject to camera distance, the angle of light incidence and the form of the subject. So, now that I've complicated matters, how do you take a meter reading? To answer that question, let's first consider the basics. Then I'll cover the complicating issues.

▼ *Here, the red letterbox is a middle-tone colour, although the white wall is around 1⅔ stops brighter than mid-tone. By using a spot meter to read the brightness of the letterbox and setting the exposure settings accordingly, a faithful exposure has been acheived, without the need for exposure compensation.*

TTL meters

Most of you will be using a built-in TTL meter and so I'll start here. The main advantage of the TTL meter is that it measures the amount of light actually entering the lens and, by default therefore, the amount of light reaching the film. A TTL meter will automatically take into account factors such as filters used and lens magnification. However, modern TTL meters come with multiple metering modes and each one needs handling differently.

Metering with TTL metering set to multi-segment metering mode

This is the most common form of light meter and takes an average of the entire scene. They are most effective when the subject brightness range of the scene is within the contrast range of the film, and the scene has a predominance of medium tones.

The technique here is much aligned to point-and-shoot. Given the above conditions the meter will give a technically accurate meter reading that you can then interpret as you wish.

▲ *Scenes where the tonality is even and contrast is relatively low are ideal examples of when to use your camera's built-in TTL-average multi-segment metering function. The averaged reading should be accurate.*

▼ *The lighting in this scene, combined with the even tones of the foliage mean that this is a good example of when to use TTL-average multi-segment metering.*

◀ *The limitation of TTL-average metering is the lack of information provided about specific areas of a scene. As such subjects with a high SBR, such as a zebra, can cause this type of system to give inaccurate results.*

Be aware, however, that the main disadvantage of this type of meter is its inability to provide any specific information about individual areas of the scene. Because of that factor, you are limited in the amount of creative control you can assert over the camera.

Metering with TTL metering set to centre-weighted metering mode

The centre-weighted setting is ideal for portraits, where the main subject fills around 75% of the frame, and where the subject brightness range (SBR) between foreground and background is within the film/PS's contrast range. The technique for metering a scene using centre-weighted metering depends on the position of the subject. That is, whether the subject is central to the image space or off-centre.

▼ *Because the main subject of the image was off-centre, I first took a meter reading from the body of the ostrich. Then, keeping the meter reading, I recomposed the image to suit my chosen composition.*

▲ *With a spot meter you can accurately assess the full SBR of a scene before calculating your preferred exposure.*

When the main subject is central to the image space frame the picture so that the main subject fills the metering circle depicted in the viewfinder and then take your meter reading. If the subject is too far away to fill the centre-metering circle then change to a longer focal length lens to meter the subject, switching back to your preferred lens before shooting. This is necessary because subject-to-camera distance affects exposure calculation. If you have no appropriate lens available then move nearer to the subject, take the meter reading and bracket +1/3 stop.

If the subject is off-centre then set the camera to the manual setting and centre the subject in the viewfinder. Then follow the process outlined above. Once you have determined your exposure and dialled in the appropriate settings, reframe the subject to its original position and take the picture.

Metering with TTL metering set to spot metering mode

Spot metering provides you with the ultimate control over exposure. A TTL spot meter will typically cover an angle of view of no more than 3°–5°. With a spot meter it is possible to measure specific parts of a scene to ascertain the true subject brightness range. The technique for spot metering is to point the metering sensor directly towards the area of the scene you want to meter. By measuring all the different tones within a scene in this way you can accurately assess the subject brightness range of the entire scene.

Hand-held meters

Hand-held meters usually offer two types of metering: reflected light metering (similar to TTL metering) and incident light metering. When operated in reflected light mode they become highly accurate spot meters, often with an angle of view of 1°. In incident light mode they measure the amount of light falling on a subject, as opposed to reflecting off a subject. The techniques for metering with the different modes are quite diverse.

Metering with a hand-held meter in reflected light spot metering mode

The principles for metering in spot metering mode with a hand-held meter are the same as for TTL metering in spot metering mode. It is important to keep the line of sight close to the camera, as the further you stray from this point the less accurate the reading will be.

The main difference is the areas covered by the hand-held meter compared to a TTL meter. Because it has such a narrow angle of view it is possible to isolate extremely small areas of the overall scene, which increases the accuracy of the meter reading. Because of this it is important to make sure that you take your meter reading from the correct area.

When using a hand-held meter it is important that you remember to take into account any external factors not automatically covered by the meter, for example, filters or high magnification lenses and accessories, such as extension tubes.

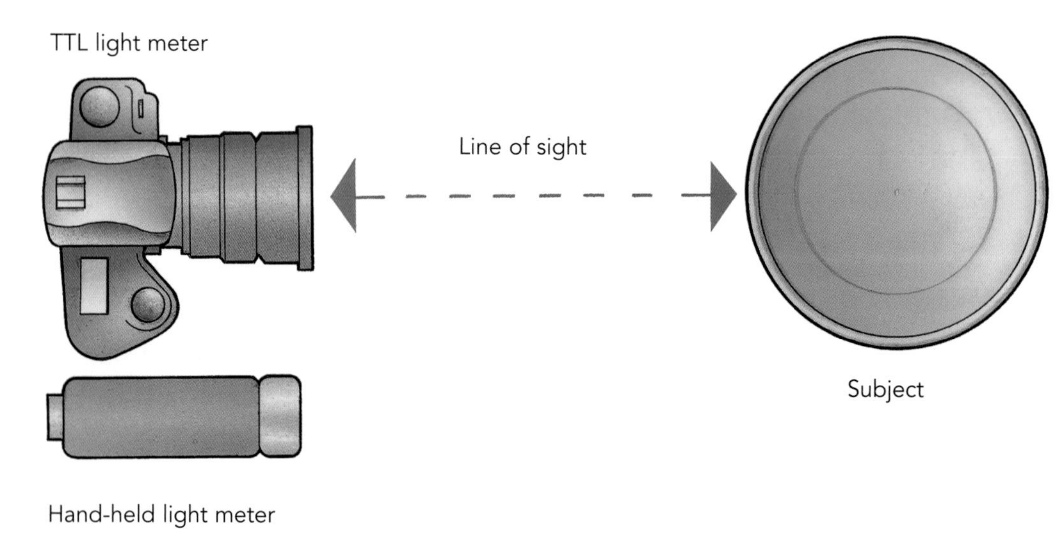

▲ *When using a hand-held reflected light meter it is important to keep the line of sight consistent with the camera.*

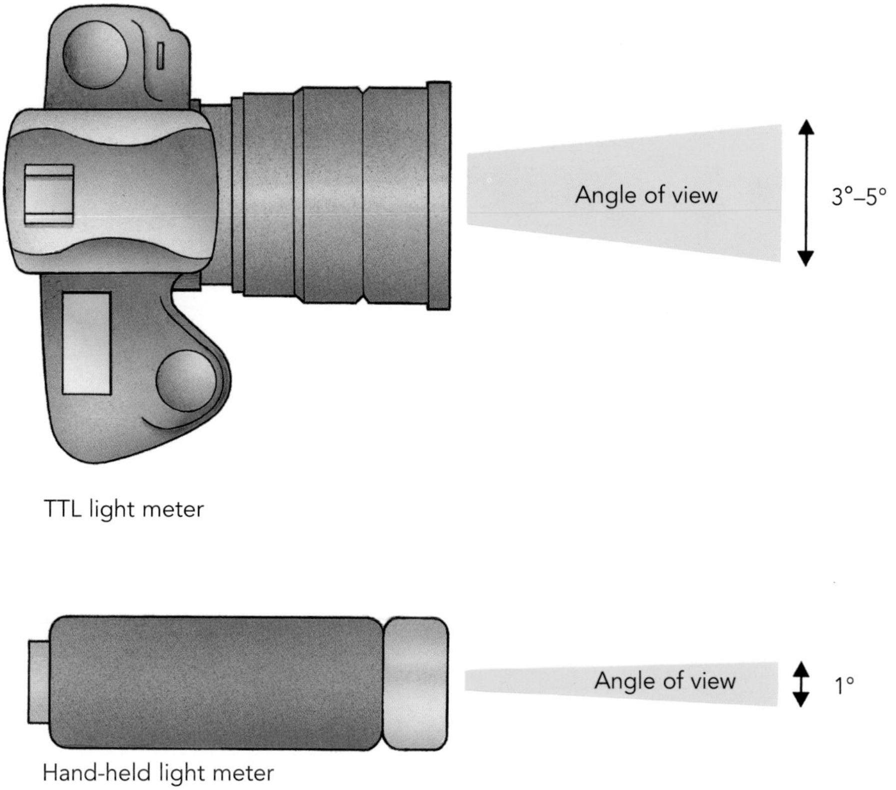

▲ *Hand-held reflected light meters often have a spot metering facility with a narrower angle of view (often 1°) than even the best in-built TTL meter.*

Metering with a hand-held meter in incident light metering mode

Incident light meters differ from reflected light meters in that they measure the light falling on a subject rather than the light reflecting back off the subject. The main advantage of this type of metering is that, unlike reflected light meters, light and dark areas within the scene do not influence the exposure values. Therefore, if you want your images to appear as they do to the naked eye you can achieve highly accurate results.

On the flip side, the main disadvantage of incident light meters is that, because they don't measure the subject brightness range, they provide little information with which you can gain creative control over the resulting photograph.

The technique for metering with this type of meter depends on the subject you are photographing. If you are able to approach the subject – say a person or a pet – then place the meter close to the subject with the invercone pointing towards the camera lens and take the meter reading.

▲ *Because of the way in which they meter, incident light meters are most effective when they are used close to the subject.*

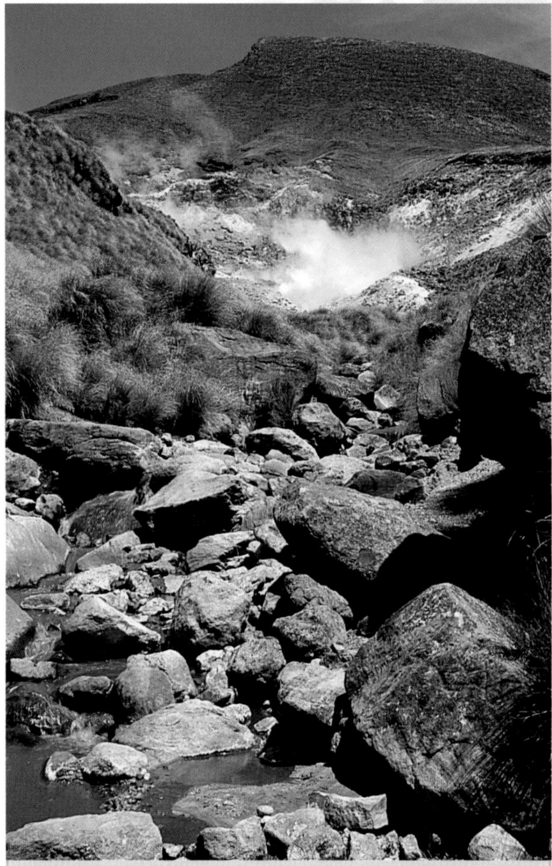

▲ *On days with bright sunshine the intensity of the light can cause an incident meter to recommend shorter shutter speeds or narrower apertures than are appropriate, causing underexposure.*

If the subject is further away or is unapproachable – such as a landscape or a wild animal – then hold the meter above your head with the dome pointing away from the camera and take the reading.

With this second approach there are some other limitations you need to bear in mind. First of all, this technique tends to fail on bright sunny days when the intensity of the light can cause the meter to give a reading that will underexpose your picture. Also, on very stormy days, when only small patches of the landscape are illuminated, the meter won't be able to read the light.

As with the hand-held reflected light meter you will still need to take into account any external factors affecting your exposures (filters, extension tubes, etc.) Remember, too, that incident light meters are also calibrated to give a medium-tone light reading and the same compensation rules apply as for reflected light meters.

► *The stormy clouds combined with the effect of the sunlight makes for complex lighting conditions. The 'patchy' quality of the light means only small sections of the landscape are illuminated. In situations such as these incident meters are less effective, and will not guarantee correct exposures.*

Complicating issues – The angle of incidence

The main factor affecting meter readings, above and beyond those already discussed is the angle between the light source and the position of the subject in relation to the camera. The brightness of a surface will alter depending on the direction you view it from in relation to the light source. To ensure a technically accurate meter reading it is important to keep the light meter as close to the line of sight between the camera and the subject. Of course, a TTL meter has the most accurate line of sight so long as the meter reading and the photograph are taken from the same spot. The series of images below illustrate this point.

Interpreting light meter readings

As I discussed earlier, all light meters are calibrated to give you an exposure value for a middle-tone subject, that is a subject that reflects 18% of the light falling on it.

When metering a medium-tone subject your light meter will give you a technically accurate exposure value. The problems start when the subject you are metering is darker than, or lighter than middle tone. Your light meter will assume all subjects are a middle tone, whatever their colour. But, the likelihood is that you will want lighter-than middle tone subjects to appear lighter than middle tone; and darker than middle-tone subjects to appear darker than middle tone. For example,

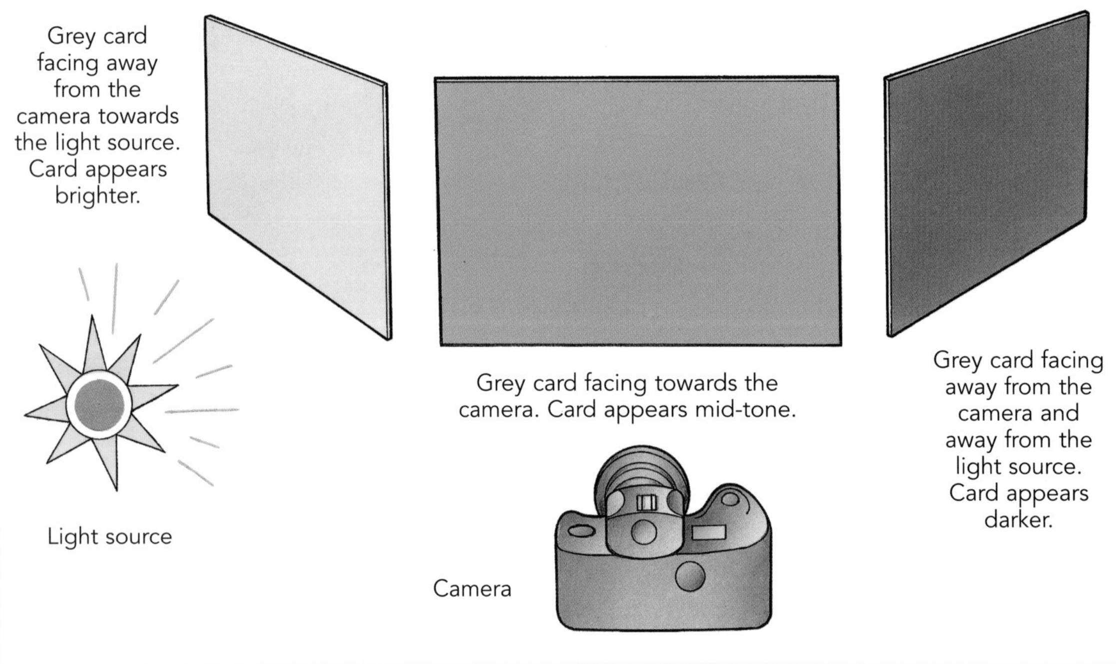
Grey card facing away from the camera towards the light source. Card appears brighter.
Light source
Grey card facing towards the camera. Card appears mid-tone.
Camera
Grey card facing away from the camera and away from the light source. Card appears darker.

▲ *The angle of incidence may effect your meter reading and it is necessary for accurate readings to keep the line of sight between meter and camera consistent.*

The middle tone

The 18% reflectance value is referred to as middle tone or medium tone because it falls exactly half way between film's ability to record pure white and pure black. For this reason it is also referred to as medium grey or 18% grey.

you would probably want snow to appear white, rather than grey. Your meter, however, will tell you only how to expose snow white as a middle-tone. Similarly, you would want a black cat to appear black. Again, though, your meter will provide you with an exposure value that indicates middle-tone – medium grey. While exposure values are often referred to in terms of grey tones the same rule applies for any colour in the visible spectrum. For example, imagine you were photographing a blue sky in the early morning. A direct meter reading would give you an exposure value equivalent to medium blue – a tone of blue you would expect to see at noon. However, in the early morning the sky will appear much lighter. In order to record it at its true tone you would need to add more light to your exposure than that indicated by the meter.

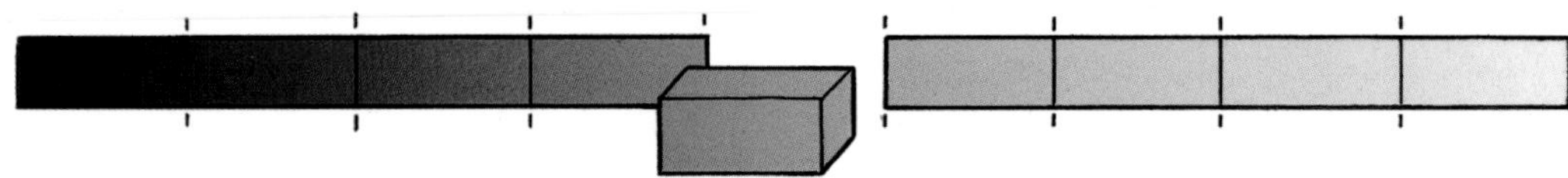

Uncompensated automatic meter reading will give a middle tone result

▲ *A meter reading of a blue sky in early morning would provide an exposure value equivalent to medium blue.*

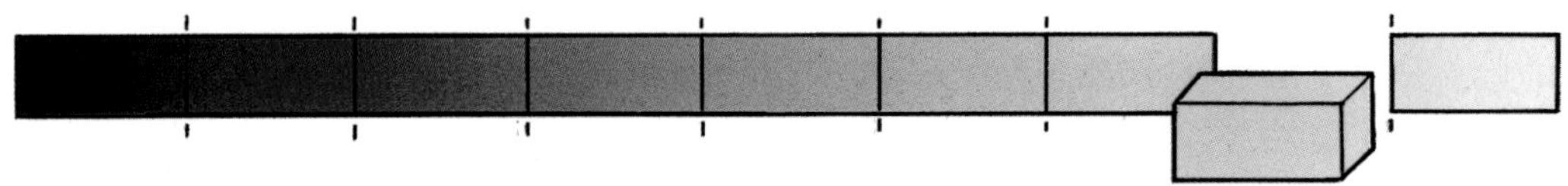

To record the early morning sky in its more natural form, in other words lighter than middle tone, you would need to increase your exposure by between 1 and 1½ stops.

▲ *A more accurate tone for early morning blue sky, however, is lighter than medium blue. Opening up the exposure by, in this case, between 1 and 1½ stops would give you the tone that more closely matches the colour of the sky.*

Try this test – A

On an overcast, dry day place three pieces of card on the ground – one white, one black and one medium grey. Set the camera's meter to autoexposure and photograph each piece of card separately, ensuring they fill the entire frame. When you review the results you will see that each photograph appears the same in tone – medium grey – as shown here.

Exposure compensation

So, when you take a meter reading you must ask yourself the question, 'Is the subject I am metering middle tone, lighter than middle tone or darker than middle tone?' If the subject is middle tone then you need make no adjustment to the exposure value given by the meter. However, if the subject is lighter than middle tone then you need to add light (open up the exposure) and if the subject is darker than middle-tone then you need to subtract light (stop down the exposure). Remember that the meter effectively underexposes lighter-than-middle tones in order to make them darker and overexposes darker-than-middle tones to make them lighter.

The next question you will be asking is, "How much compensation should I apply for different subjects?" The chart below can be used as a guide.

You may have noticed that throughout this section I have referred to everything in terms of a grey scale – as illustrated above. This is because all light meters, with the exception of the Nikon F5, 'see' everything as a grey scale – they do not recognize colours. This makes life a

Try this test – B

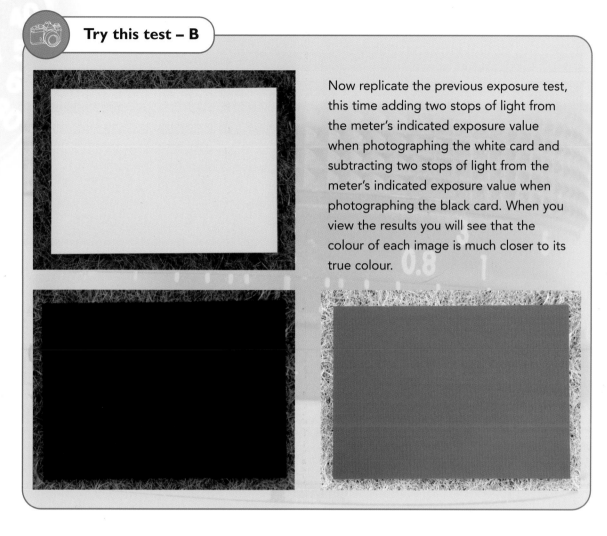

Now replicate the previous exposure test, this time adding two stops of light from the meter's indicated exposure value when photographing the white card and subtracting two stops of light from the meter's indicated exposure value when photographing the black card. When you view the results you will see that the colour of each image is much closer to its true colour.

little complicated for you as the photographer because you see everything in colour. Therefore, in order to interpret the tones accurately in any scene, you must be able to match colour tones to the grey scale. To help you along the way I have provided some guidance in the chart above. Remember that these figures are approximations and should always be tested using your own equipment and film/PS.

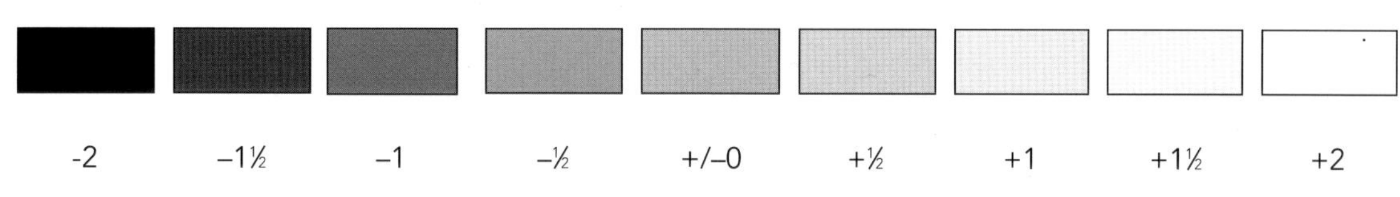

▼ *Cameras see everything in terms of a grey scale, as shown here. Levels of exposure compensation for different tones are indicated for guidance.*

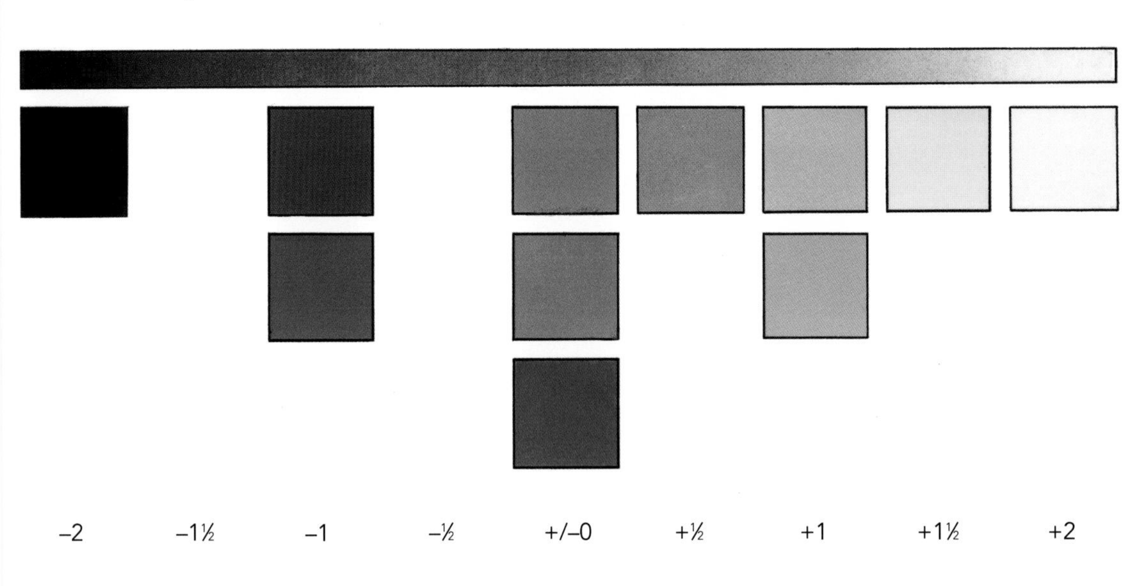

▲ *Different colours reflect different levels of light and in order to render the colours correctly in the final exposure you must compensate accordingly. The values given here can be used as an exposure guide.*

Applying exposure settings

Now that you have identified your required exposure settings the next step in the process is deciding which combination of settings to use. I have already identified lens aperture and shutter speed as the two main tools for managing exposure. What you have to decide is which of the two gets priority.

Lens aperture

One of the decisions you have to make when making a photograph is what's the 'story' you are trying to tell? For example, are you trying to give the subject a sense of place? Or are you trying to place an emphasis on and to isolate a particular part of a scene? How a viewer 'reads' the pictures you make should be determined by you not by the camera, and one of the mechanisms you have available to take control over the creative aspects of image making is lens aperture. Lens aperture affects the amount of depth of field you have to work with and depth of field influences the way we perceive a scene or subject. In the example facing, the larger image has used a very narrow depth of field (wide aperture) to place the emphasis on the animal and its behaviour. In this image it is impossible to tell where the leopard is as the photograph provides no information about sense of place. In the smaller image, however, I have used a small aperture to increase depth of field, making more of the overall scene sharp, resulting in far more information about the animal's surroundings. In this image it becomes obvious where the picture was taken.

◀ *In this image, a large depth of field makes the animal's surroundings more obvious. This is useful if you want to place a subject in a wider context. Showing an animal in its natural habitat can add an extra level of interest for the viewer and also adds variety to your portfolio.*

▼ *By selecting a wide aperture, depth of field is greatly reduced, which can help to disguise an unsightly background. In this case the wire mesh of the enclosure is no longer visible as the depth of field is too shallow to render anything other than the leopard's face sharp on film.*

Depth of field

Depth of field is also affected by focal length and distance to subject. In order to calculate the exact depth of field, given all three variations, you need to refer to depth of field charts, usually provided with the lens. Some cameras have depth of field preview that allows you to see exactly the available depth of field in any given scene.

Shutter speed

The other creative decision you have to make is how you represent motion in your pictures, and motion is controlled via shutter speed. A fast shutter speed will freeze the action of motion giving a more static appearance to the subject. Using a slow shutter speed will have the opposite effect, blurring the edges of the subject giving a sense of movement. Look at the two sample images below of a waterfall and note how changing the shutter speed affects the way the motion of the water is recorded.

Camera shake

Shutter speed may also take priority if you are hand-holding the camera. In this instance a fast shutter speed will help to minimize camera shake.

▼ *A fast shutter speed (here 1/100sec) will freeze motion, this will show subject detail although the image may look static.*

▼ *A slow shutter speed (here 1/10sec) will blur motion. This can help to create a greater sense of visual energy in the final image, and convey how a subject moves.*

Bracketing

Despite your best efforts it is sometimes impossible to calculate exposure values faithfully. Many factors can cause you to misjudge an exposure, such as very bright sunlight reflecting off shiny surfaces (e.g. water, sand and glass), constantly changing light conditions, and subtle variations in a subject's tonality. Consider, too, that film manufacturers and processing laboratories operate to tolerance levels that could make a difference of up to a 1/2 stop in your exposures.

For this reason it is often advisable to bracket your exposures. That is, take more than one photograph of the same scene at varying exposure values above and below your initial exposure setting. Typically, the variance should be around a 1/3–1/2 stop. On rare occasions you may want to go as far as +/–1 stop.

▶ *The three images here show bracketing at work. The first image was taken at -1/2 stop, the middle image at the given meter reading, and the third image at +1/2 stop. In this instance the original reading proved to be the most accurate.*

Digital capture – bracketing

The advent of digital capture has made bracketing less essential through instant replay of images. However, even with digital technology bracketing has a role to play. Consider a scene that involves a fast-moving subject, such as a racing car or a cheetah chasing an antelope. On these occasions time will not allow for you to check the exposure in the screen and then go back to try the shot again if the resulting image isn't what you had planned. Also, the digital screen on the camera is not always a true reflection of the actual brightness value of the image.

What to do when ...

Of course, if exposure were as simple as all that then there would be little need for a book like this. In reality, the interaction between light and subject can often become quite complex. While the ability to obtain faithful exposures under normal conditions will improve the consistency of your image making, your ability to handle extreme conditions will ensure that you are able to take advantage of all the photo opportunities that come your way.

◀ *Learning to handle complex lighting conditions will help you make consistently good pictures.*

Westonbirt Arboretum, Gloucestershire, UK.

35mm panoramic camera, 45mm lens, Fuji Velvia, 1/250sec at f/11

◀ *The following four images were all taken using the 'sunny f/16' rule. Work each exposure setting back to f/16 and all the shutter speeds will equal 1/50sec – the ISO rating of Fuji Velvia is 50.*

Stirling Falls, Milford Sound, New Zealand.

35mm panoramic camera, 45mm lens, Fuji Velvia, 1/200sec at f/8

Photographing in bright sunlight

In extremely bright conditions on a clear day lighter-than- and darker-than-middle tone subjects can easily fool your camera's meter. Any exposure compensation you apply will be ineffective if the original meter reading was off the mark. The solution to this problem is to use the 'sunny f/16' rule. Despite the millions of dollars invested by the camera manufacturers in designing the ultimate light meter, sometimes the simple solutions are the best solutions. The 'sunny f/16' rule works by setting your lens aperture at f/16 and your shutter speed at the setting closest to that of the ISO rating of the film you're using. For example, if you're using Fuji Provia 100F, then your exposure setting using the 'sunny f/16' rule would be f/16 at 1/100sec (or 1/125sec if your camera doesn't allow 1/3 stop adjustments). Once you have this base setting you can then use any equivalent combination of settings. In the above example, for instance, you could also use 1/200sec (1/250sec) at f/11 or 1/50sec (1/60sec) at f/22. If you don't believe me, try it! The following images were taken using that calculation.

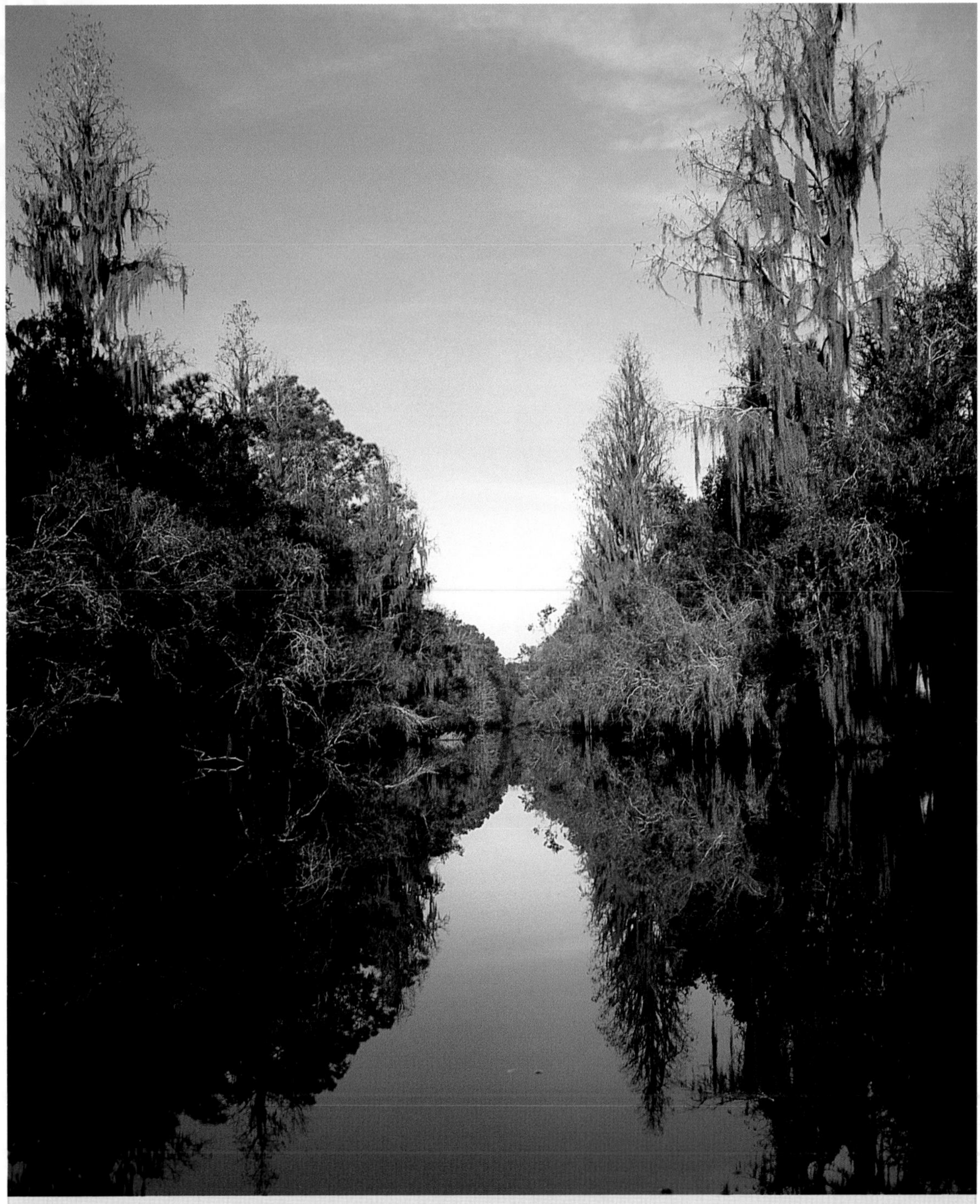

▲ *Okefenokee National Wildlife Refuge, Georgia, USA.*

35mm camera, 50mm lens, Fuji Velvia, 1/50sec at f/16

◀ *Tongariro Pass, Tongariro National Park, New Zealand.*

35mm camera, 28mm lens, Fuji Velvia, 1/25sec at f/22

▼ *Lindisfarne Castle, Lindisfarne, Northumberland, UK.*

35mm camera, 24mm lens, Fuji Velvia, 1/12sec at f/32

Photographing white subjects in bright conditions

▲ *The 'sunny f/16' often fails with a white subject on a bright day. This image of the Franz Joseph Glacier on New Zealand's South Island was taken using the alternative 'sunny f/22' rule.*

35mm camera, 200mm lens, Fuji Provia 100F, 1/400sec at f/11

One time when the 'sunny f/16' rule is less effective is when photographing white subjects under very bright conditions, when the subject fills a large portion of the picture frame. Under these circumstances using the f/16 setting would result in losing detail in the highlights – something best avoided if at all possible. You would encounter a similar problem when including highly reflective, shiny surfaces such as sand, snow or water.

A variation of the 'sunny f/16' rule is the 'sunny f/22' rule. It works in exactly the same way except your base lens aperture setting is f/22. Reducing the level of light reaching the film by half will darken the highlight areas of the image and add detail. As with the 'sunny f/16' rule, once you have determined the correct shutter speed at f/22 you can use any equivalent combination of settings for your final exposure.

▲ *The two images on this page are further examples of where to use the 'sunny f/22' rule to reproduce white faithfully.*

Mount Cook Range, South Island, New Zealand.

35mm camera, 400mm lens, Fuji Velvia, 1/200sec at f/11

◄ *White heron, Mkuzi National Park, Kwa-Zulu Natal, South Africa.*

35mm camera, 800mm lens, Fuji Provia 100F, 1/800sec at f/8

Photographing backlit subjects

You probably remember the age-old advice, 'always photograph with the sun behind you'. Fortunately, the photographic art has moved on since that phrase was coined and light is now used far more creatively. One of the most difficult lighting situations to meter for is shooting into the light, where your subject is backlit. The light coming from behind the subject fools the meter and you end up with an underexposed image, where the surface facing the camera – that is, the surface you're photographing – loses all detail.

▼ *Cropping right in on a backlit subject makes exposure simpler. Here I wanted to accentuate the colour of the Japanese maple leaves, so I exposed for the red and closed down one stop to help saturate the colours and to account for the bright sunlight shining through.*

35mm camera, 120mm lens, Fuji Velvia, 1/30sec at f/5.6

Getting close to the subject so that it fills the frame will overcome the problem but this is not always possible. The best solution to this dilemma is to use a spot meter and to meter only the surface area facing you. Because the spot meter has a very narrow angle of view the bright backlighting won't influence it. If your camera has no spot meter you can improvise by attaching a long telephoto lens and using centre-weighted metering instead.

If all else fails, backlighting is one condition where the hand-held incident light meter is worth its weight in gold. Hold the meter above your head and in front of you with the invercone (white dome) facing towards the camera. The meter will then read the light falling on the surface in shadow.

▼ *Shooting up into the sun, I took a spot meter reading of the underside of these giant fern trees, which were a middle-tone green.*

35mm camera, 28mm lens, Fuji Velvia, 1/25sec at f/8

▲ *Silhouettes are both effective and easily achieved. For this picture of a lone oak tree, I took a meter reading from the sky just above the hedge on the right and opened up one stop.*

35mm camera, 300mm lens, Fuji Velvia, 1 sec at f/11

Photographing silhouettes

Sometimes when photographing into the light you purposefully want the subject to be underexposed in order to create a silhouette. Silhouettes are very powerful images and demonstrate my principle that there is no such thing as correct exposure. When creating a silhouette you should do the complete opposite to what I've just advised for photographing backlit subjects. What you are trying to achieve is the removal of any detail on the surface in shadow. Take a meter reading from an area behind the subject but excluding the light source itself. Then take a spot meter reading of the subject. If the difference between the two readings is greater than the contrast range of the film/PS then the shadow will show no detail and be rendered, in the final image, as a silhouette.

Warning

Never look directly into the sun, either with the naked eye or through a camera.

▲ *For these images I used the same technique, taking a reading from the light part of the sky and opening up one stop.*

35mm panoramic camera, 45mm lens, Fuji Velvia, 1/2sec at f/8

▼ *35mm camera, 24mm lens, Fuji Velvia, 1 sec at f/22*

▲ *The hours in between sunset and night can produce some very evocative images.*

35mm camera, 300mm lens, Fuji Velvia, 1 sec at f/5.6

Photographing in low light

When photographing in low light conditions the same exposure calculation rules apply as for any other lighting conditions. The problem you are likely to encounter is when the light gets so low that it is beyond the sensitivity range of the meter. There are two possible solutions to this problem and, again, the hand-held incident light meter may come to your rescue.

The dome on an incident light meter removes around 80% of the light falling on it. Remove it and this 'lost' light is allowed to reach the metering cell. This may be enough to get the meter back above its sensitivity threshold. If it is then take an incident light reading as normal (described on page 79) and then set 1/5 of the indicated exposure as your medium-tone setting. (The 1/5 calculation replicates the use of the now removed dome.)

The other alternative is to use your experience and a bit of guesswork. If the light illuminating your subject is too low to meter look for a brighter area of the scene and meter from that, most likely using a spot meter. Then, estimate the difference between the brightness value and adjust the meter reading accordingly.

Low light – bracketing

In these types of conditions, when your exposure calculations are subject to estimations and guesswork, it is always advisable to bracket your exposures (described on page 89).

Using very slow shutter speeds

There are numerous circumstances that will dictate you working at long shutter speeds (greater than one second). Low light is one example. Using slow film or low ISO equivalency on a digital SLR, or shooting at minimum apertures are others.

The law of reciprocity is that a change in one exposure setting can be compensated for by an equal and opposite change in another.

▼ *With exposures longer than one second you fall foul of the law of reciprocity failure. To capture Eilean Donan Castle in Scotland I increased my original setting of 4 sec at f/22 by a 1/2 stop to 6 sec at f/22 in order to take account of the decreasing sensitivity of the film.*

▲ *In high-contrast situations like this it is best to experiment a bit and see what works for you.*

35mm panoramic camera, 90mm lens, Fuji Provia 100F, 15 sec at f/8

However, due to the way film emulsion reacts to long-time exposures this law no longer applies once your shutter speed exceeds one second. In a nutshell, film sensitivity decreases the longer it is exposed to light. So, for example, if you were working with an exposure setting of f/11 at two seconds and decided to alter the lens aperture to f/16 to gain additional depth of field, normally you would simply reduce the shutter speed to four seconds to compensate. However, if you did just that the resulting image may be underexposed. This reaction is referred to as reciprocity law failure and must be compensated for when shooting at slow shutter speeds. The table below indicates the degree of compensation required for some of the most popular film types.

▲ *Photographing a full moon on a clear night I have found an exposure setting of 1/30sec at f/11 on ISO 100 film usually works well.*

Table 8 – Reciprocity law failure compensation for popular film types

Make of film:

FUJI	**1 sec**	**4 sec**	**16 sec**	**64 sec**
Fuji Velvia (RVP)	None	+1/3 stop	+2/3 stop	Not advised
Fuji Provia 100F (RDP III)	None	None	None	None
Fuji Astia 100 (RAP)	None	None	None	+1/3 stop
Fuji Provia 400F (RHP III)	None	None	None	+2/3 stop
Fuji Sensia 100 (RA)	None	None	none	+2/3 stop
Fuji Sensia 200 (RM)	None	None	None	+2/3 stop

KODAK	**1 sec**	**10 sec**	**100 sec**
Ektachrome E100VS (Pro)	None	None	None
Ektachrome E100SW (pro)	None	None	Not advised
Kodachrome 64	Not advised	Not advised	Not advised
Kodachrome 200	+1/2 stop	Not advised	Not advised
ELITE chrome 400 (EL)	+1/3–1/2 stop	+1/2 stop	Not advised
PORTRA (Pro) 160NC/160VC/400NC/ 400VC/400UC	None	None	Not advised
SUPRA (Pro) 100/400/800	Not advised	Not advised	Not advised

▲▶ *The tables above and opposite are the manufacturers' recommended guidelines and I would suggest testing them to increase accuracy levels.*

Colour shifts

The other problem caused when taking pictures with colour film and using long-time exposures is colour shifts. Colour shifts are caused because the separate layers of emulsion react differently to reciprocity failure. Because of this it is advised that you use colour correction filters. The filters recommended are listed in the table below.

Table 9 – Colour compensation for long exposures of popular film types

FUJI	**1 sec**	**4 sec**	**16 sec**	**64 sec**
Fuji Velvia (RVP)	None	5M	10M	Not advised
Fuji Provia 100F (RDP III)	None	None	None	None
Fuji Astia 100 (RAP)	None	None	None	None
Fuji Provia 400F (RHP III)	None	None	None	5G
Fuji Sensia 100 (RA)	None	None	None	None
Fuji Sensia 200 (RM)	None	None	None	5G
KODAK		**1 sec**	**10 sec**	**100 sec**
Ektachrome E100VS (Pro)		None	None	None
Ektachrome E100SW (Pro)		None	None	075Y
Kodachrome 64		Not advised	Not advised	Not advised
Kodachrome 200		10Y	Not advised	Not advised
ELITE chrome 400 (EL)		05R	10R	Not advised
PORTRA (Pro) 160NC/160VC/400NC/400VC/400UC		None	None	Not advised
SUPRA (Pro) 100/400/800		Not advised	Not advised	Not advised

Photographing high-contrast scenes

If everything in photography worked on the law of averages then our lives would be much simpler. Unfortunately, life's not like that and we are often presented with scenes that are far from average. The human eye is an exceptional tool and we can distinguish detail in light and dark objects with a great deal of latitude. Photographic film and digital PSs, on the other hand, have very limited latitude and, when deciding how to expose for a certain scene, you must be aware of, and make account for these limitations.

The range between the subjects' darkest and lightest areas is known as the subject brightness range (SBR). When calculating exposure values you must first determine the degree of variation. To help in this exercise we can use a modification of the zone system, devised by the great American photographic pioneer, Ansel Adams.

The grey scale, reproduced below, is a graphic representation of how the real world appears in grey tones. When inventing the zone system, Adams divided the scale into nine distinct and equal segments. (This was later extended to eleven zones although, for the purpose of this book, I shall concentrate on the original nine, the eleven-zone system being recommended only for large-format photography.)

So how does this work in practice? Using the grey scale, for each of the tones visible in the scene you are photographing, you can identify which zone they fall into. Once you have applied a zone for each part of the scene you will have identified the SBR. To illustrate this, look at the facing page.

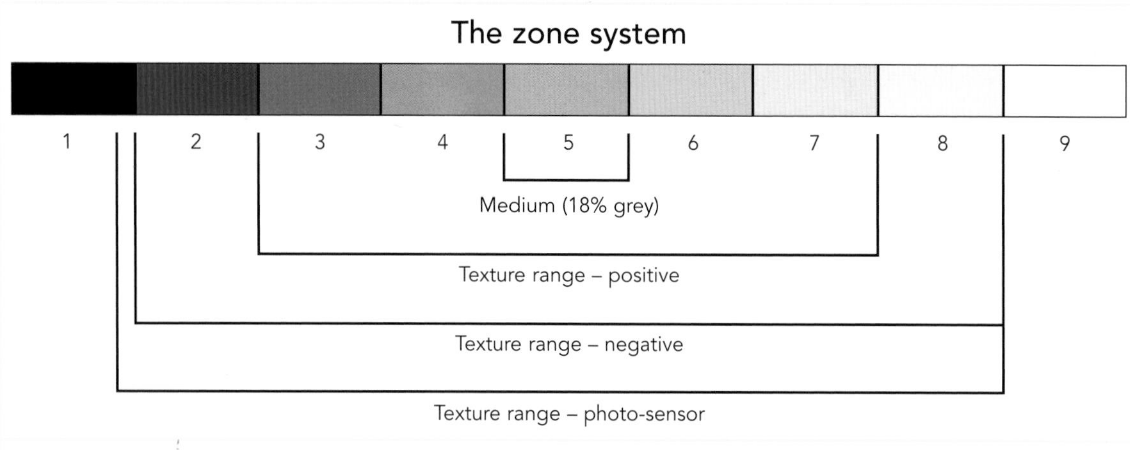

▲ *To help relate the grey scale to exposure calculation each segment has an identifying number, 1 being pure black and 9 being pure white. Starting from zone 1, the centre of each segment is exactly twice as bright as the previous segment and equals a one-stop difference in exposure value. The middle segment – zone 5 – is medium grey and is the equivalent of the 18% grey that all light meters are calibrated to record.*

▼ *Compare this image with the overlay I made at the time (shown overleaf). The brightness range in this scene is around eight stops, three stops greater than the latitude of the film I was using. So, I had to make a decision as to whether I would render detail in the shadow areas or the highlight areas. In this instance I exposed for the shadows. Compare this final picture with the overlay on page 108. It clearly shows that the brightness range is greater than the film's latitude; this helped me to decide on the way in which to expose the image, to achieve the results I wanted.*

I have applied a zone value to each part of the scene, where the tone varies in brightness. You can now see that the darkest part of the scene falls into zone 2 and the brightest part of the scene falls into zone 9. This gives me a SBR of eight stops – far in excess of the latitude of slide film and even outside that of print film and digital CCD. What this exercise allows me to do is pre-visualize the final image and to make the necessary adjustments in-camera to achieve an SBR within the latitude of the film I am using or, as in this case, to make a decision on whether to expose for the highlights or shadow areas.

► *Compare this overlay to the final image on page 107. It shows you how I decided to expose the scene given the limitations of the film's latitude in comparison with the wider SBR of the scene. (Also see page 106 for further explanation of the Zone System)*

▼ *In scenes with high levels of contrast sometimes you have to decide whether to expose for the highlights or the shadows. Typically, it is better to expose for highlights as underexposed shadows look better to us than overexposed highlights, but there are some exceptions.*

Using photographic filters

The art of photography is a combination of graphic design and managing light. In the latter of these two disciplines, light management, essential tools are filters. While there are many types of filter available some are used far more frequently than others and it is these that I will concentrate on in the following section.

The issue that you will face when photographing using a filter is how much light the filter absorbs. As a rule of thumb, the darker the filter the more light is lost. If you are metering with a TTL meter then the problems are somewhat negated. Because the camera is measuring the amount of light actually entering the lens it will automatically take into account any filters you have in place... in theory. As with every rule, however, there are exceptions, which I'll explain in a moment.

The following table indicates the level of exposure compensation required for some of the more popular single-tone filters, when metered with a non-TTL meter. When using a TTL meter the meter will automatically compensate for the light absorbance of the filters listed in this table.

Not all filters are single tone and these need more thought when calculating exposure. By far the most complex filter is the polarizing filter, used particularly by landscape photographers. The linear-type polarizing filter is also the exception to the rule I mentioned above.

▼ *I compensated by +1/3 stop for the 81B filter enhancing the Dorset coast's early morning glow.*

645 camera, 6mm lens, Fuji Velvia, 81B filter, 3 sec at f/32

Table 10 – Single-tone filters

Colour	**81A**	**81B**	**81C**	**81D**	**B&W**	
81 series 'warm'	+1/3	+1/3	+1/3	+2/3	Light Red	+2
Colour	**82A**	**82B**	**82C**	**82D**	Yellow	+1/3
82 series	+1/3	+1/3	+2/3	+2/3	Orange	+1
					Yellow/Green	+1⅓

Polarizing filters

There are two types of polarizing filters – linear and circular. A TTL meter will automatically compensate for any light loss when using a circular polarizer. However, because of the design of the linear-type polarizer even a TTL meter will be baffled.

The purpose of a polarizing filter is to block polarized light from entering the lens, and subsequently from reaching the photographic recording material. Depending on the position of the filter it will block more, or less light, which ultimately affects the amount of exposure compensation required.

When using a linear-type polarizer and/or metering with a non-TTL meter, use the following table to calculate the amount of exposure compensation required. These values should be used as a guide only and because calculating exposure when using a polarizing filter is not an exact science I would recommend bracketing a 1/3 or 1/2 stop either side.

Table 11 – Polarizing filters

Polarization	Exposure compensation
1/4	½ stop
1/2	1 stop
3/4	1½ stops
Full	2 stops

▼ *A polarizing filter helped to saturate the colour of this emerald lake in Tongariro National Park, New Zealand. At full polarization I added two stops of light to the exposure settings and bracketed a 1/2 stop either side, just to be safe.*

35mm panoramic camera, 45mm lens, Fuji Velvia, polarizing filter, 1/60sec at f/16

Graduated neutral density filters

▲ *To even the tones between the sky and the foreground I added a neutral density graduated 0.6 filter (2 stops) to this scene. Without it the sky would have become washed out and lacking in detail.*

Graduated neutral density (GND) filters are most often used in landscape photography where frequently the difference in tone between the sky and the land is quite pronounced. When this difference is outside the latitude of the film or PS you will lose detail in either the bright or shadow areas. For example, if you meter for the sky the landscape itself will come out underexposed and if you meter for the landscape the sky will be overexposed. GND filters prevent this by allowing you to darken the sky without changing its natural colour, so that its brightness is closer to the tone of the landscape. Because the SBR depends on the scene NDG filters come in different strengths between one and three stops in 1/2 stop increments. They can also be used together to achieve strengths beyond three stops.

▲ *The SBR between the sky and the foreground in this photograph was quite intense. I added a NDG 0.9 together with a NDG 0.3, giving me a total of four stops' strength – and still some of the sky has been overexposed.*

Table 12 – f/stop index

Filter type	Strength
NDG 0.3	1 stop
NDG 0.45	1½ stops
NDG 0.6	2 stops
NDG 0.75	2½ stops
NDG 0.9	3 stops

When using a GND filter with a TTL meter you must meter the scene without the filter in place in front of the lens. Metering with the filter in front of the lens will give a technically inaccurate reading and defeat the object of its use. You will also need to ensure that the camera is set to manual exposure mode. The technique for calculating the strength of GND filter required is outlined below:

1. Take a meter reading for the landscape and place it in the appropriate zone on the grey scale.
2. Then, take a meter reading for the sky and, again, place it in the appropriate zone on the grey scale.
3. The number of zones between the two marks will indicate the difference in stops. You can then use this knowledge to decide the strength of filter needed to even out the two tones.

▼ *So, for example, let's say that you meter the landscape and your meter's reading indicates a zone value of 5 – medium tone (see illustration X).*

Next, the meter reading for the sky indicates a zone value of 8 (see illustration Y).

The difference in SBR is three zones, which is equal to three stops. So, by placing a three stop NDG filter over the area of sky you effectively even the tones across the image, in this example, placing the sky in zone 5, the same zone as the landscape. (see illustration Z).

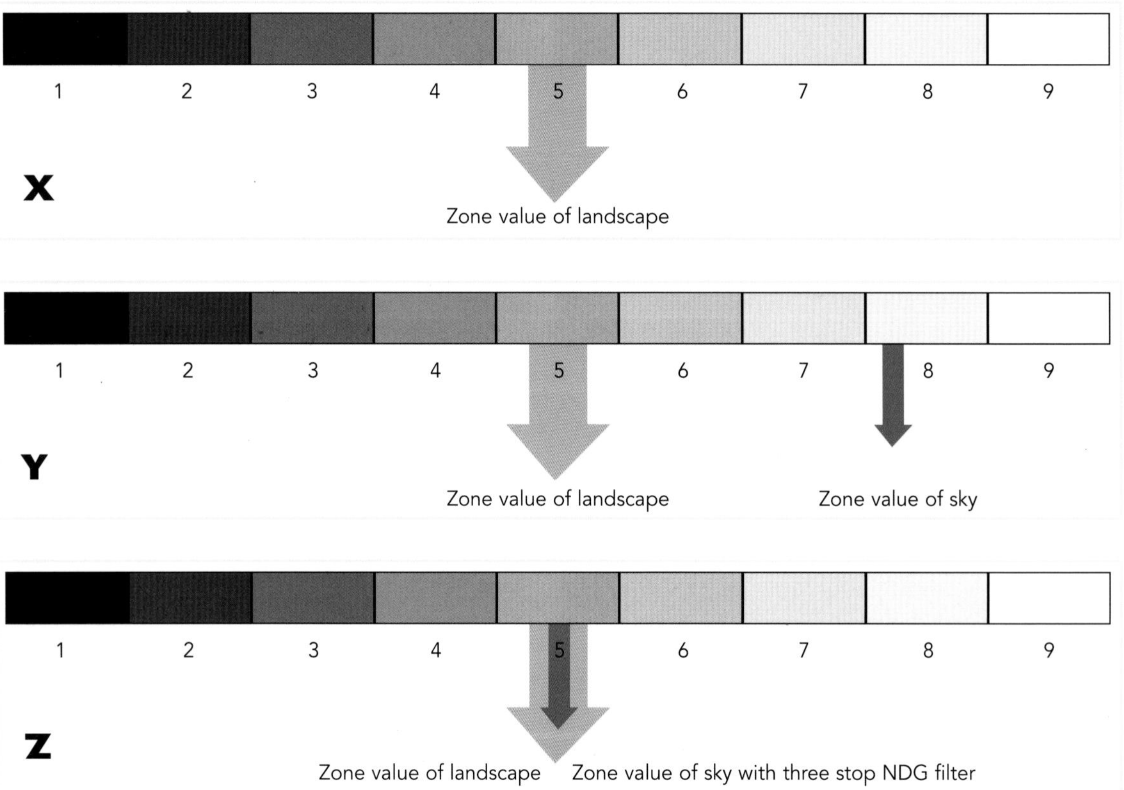

Photographing close-ups

Macro and close-up photography often involves the use of extenders, either in the form of extension tubes or bellows. While these accessories allow you to focus more closely to your subject they also reduce the amount of light reaching the film/PS, which, in turn, affects your exposure – and the longer the extension the greater the reduction in light. It's very much like a tunnel: the further into the tunnel you travel the less light there is.

◄ *Correctly exposing to avoid black backgrounds when photographing close-up images requires skill. Using fill-in flash with daylight, together with the slow-sync flash application helps to balance the foreground and background.*

35mm camera, 105mm macro lens, Fuji Velvia, 1/30sec at f/22

▲ *In this image the sunlight shining through the centre of the flower has created a bright highlight causing the subject to have an SBR outside the latitude of the film.*

35mm camera, 105mm macro lens, Fuji Velvia, 1/125sec at f/22

◀ *TTL metering works in exactly the same way for close-up photography as it does for normal photography, and will automatically take into account any accessories used, such as extension tubes.*

35mm camera, 50mm lens, extension tubes, Fuji Velvia, 1/60sec at f/16

Metering for close-ups using a TTL meter overcomes any problems you may otherwise face because it automatically compensates for the loss of light. Using a TTL meter in close-up work means you can meter as for any other subject.

If you are using a hand-held meter or, indeed, the 'sunny f/16' rule then you will need to calculate the level of compensation required. This is best done by determining the relevant extension/compensation factors for the close-up equipment you are using. To calculate the necessary exposure compensation copy the following steps:

▶ *First focus your lens at infinity. If you have an autofocus camera the best way to do this is by switching to manual focus and using the focusing ring yourself.*

◀ *Attach your camera to a tripod to maintain a constant distance.*

▶ *Now point your camera at an even surface, such as a wall. It is important that the surface is not just even in shape, but also in tone. This means that the level of light falling on it must be consistant.*

For example, say your first meter reading was 1/125sec at f/8 and your second meter reading was 1/90sec at f/8. The difference between the two readings is 1/2 stop. Now, every time you use that extension tube with the lens set at infinity you know to add an extra 1/2 stop of light. To calculate the exposure compensation factor for other close-up extension accessories, repeat the process.

So what happens if you focus your lens at its minimum focusing distance? Well, the same issues apply. Because you have extended the distance between the front of the lens and the film plane/PS you are reducing the amount of light reaching the film. To calculate the compensation factor for your lens you need to run another test.

◀ *Take a meter reading from the even surface. Your first meter reading will be taken as the base of your calculations (write this down as you don't want to go through the whole process again).*

▶ *Without moving the camera to subject distance, set the lens to its closest focusing distance – if you want to find the lens compensation factor – or add an extension tube – if you want to find the extension tube compensation factor. It's ivery mportant that the camera remains still while you do this.*

◀ *Now take a new meter reading and record the change in exposure. The difference between your first exposure and second exposure is the compensation factor for that lens or extension tube.*

Using the example described above, let's now assume you want to crop right in and you set the lens to its nearest focusing distance. To calculate the exposure compensation factor simply add the two values together. For example, if the compensation factor for your extension tube is 1/2 stop and the compensation factor for your lens is one stop, then the total compensation factor will be 1½ stops.

Of course, if you are using different lenses then you will need to repeat these processes with each lens you intend to use. Once done, however, you can keep an 'Exposure Compensation Record Card' and use it on subsequent shoots.

Flash exposure

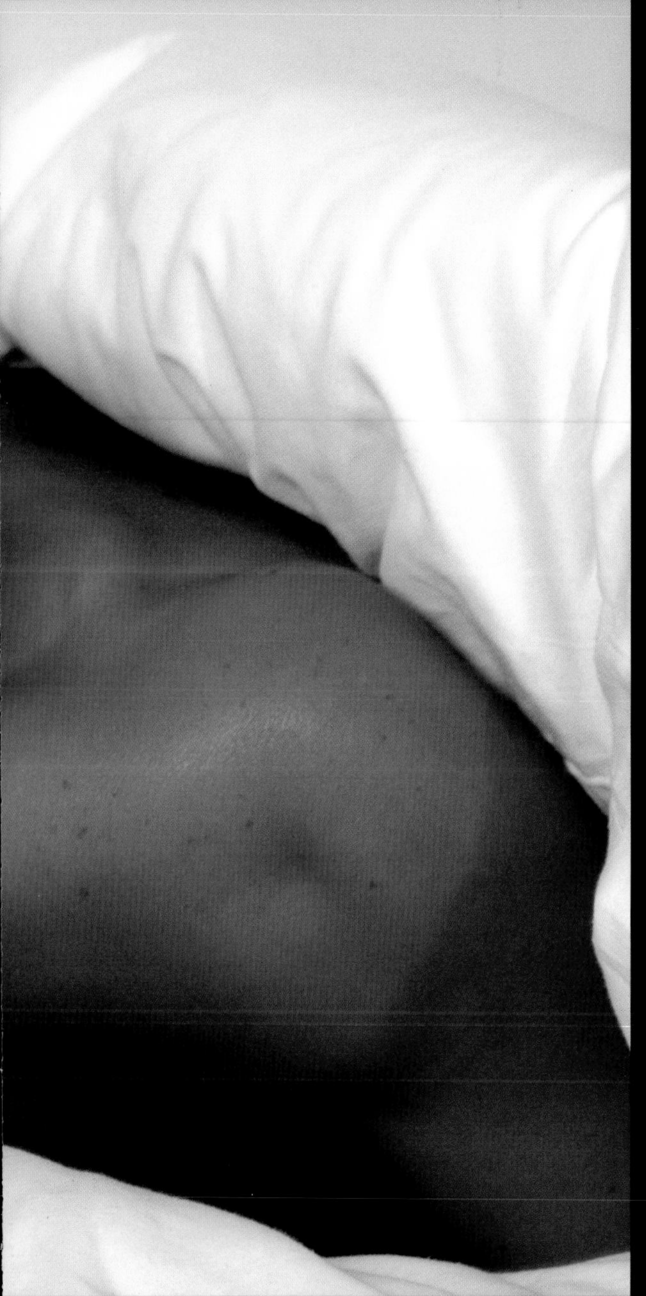

So far, I have concentrated on calculating exposure under natural light conditions. So what happens when you add your own light source into the equation?

◀ *Working in a studio allows you to play God with light but, once again, it is how you control exposure that adds sparkle to your pictures.*

35mm digital camera, 80mm lens, 1/125sec at f/8.

TTL-flash metering

Today's dedicated flash units are extremely sophisticated and the camera's TTL-flash metering systems highly accurate. This doesn't just apply to the top end of the market. Many cheaper flash units and metering systems have benefited from the advances made with professional models.

In the past, flash units would discharge at full power irrespective of the circumstances. This would leave all of the flash exposure calculations in the hands of the photographer. Now that has changed and most modern systems work by discharging only the correct amount of light given your exposure settings and the prevailing shooting conditions.

However, as with non-flash TTL metering the amount of light discharged is set to render your subject mid-tone. And, as I've already discussed, this may not be appropriate if you don't want your subjects to appear mid-tone. So how do you go about compensating for flash exposure?

Well, first of all you may find that your flash unit or your camera allows you to set a compensation factor to flash exposure settings in much the same way as you do for your non-flash exposures. If this is the case then you can use the same colour scales, to determine the amount of compensation that you need to render a subject the correct tone, that appear on page 86.

▼ *The eagle owl pictured below is a darker-than-mid-tone subject, being approximately one stop darker than the 18% average. If I had taken this photograph with the flash unit set to zero compensation, then the resulting image would have appeared lighter (as illustrated by the inset image). To get the exposure right I had to add minus one stop compensation, which reduced the amount of light emitted by the flash unit resulting in a faithful exposure of the owl's feathers and, most importantly, its eyes.*

Manual flash exposure calculation

If you are working with less sophisticated flash and camera systems then you will need to understand how to calculate flash exposure manually, rather than leave it to chance.

Flash exposure is calculated using the flash-to-subject distance, as opposed to camera-to-subject distance (which is how you calculate non-flash exposure). Of course when you use a flash unit mounted on the camera's hotshoe these distances will be the same. If the flash is too far away from the subject then too little, or even no light, will reach it and the final image will come out underexposed. So what you need to do is get the subject within range of the flash unit. The question is, 'How do you work out what that range is?'

Firstly, you will need to know what the guide number (GN) of your flash unit is. The guide number is given by the manufacturer and refers to the maximum operating distance of the flash unit at a given ISO. The guide number is normally given for ISO 100 film.

Once you know the guide number and the base ISO rating then it is a simple step to calculate the guide number for different film speeds. To do this it is best to work in stops, unless you are a mathematical wizard, using the f/stop series of numbers. For example, let's say your flash has a guide number of 160 for ISO 400 film. To calculate the guide number for, say, Fuji Velvia 50 film, first calculate the difference in stops in film speed. Fuji Velvia 50 is three stops slower than ISO 400 film. For the purpose of calculation, drop the zero from the original guide number (160) giving you 16 and apply this to the f/stop scale: f/16. Now, open up three stops from f/16 (because of the slower film speed) and

▲ *If the flash unit is too far from the subject then too little light will cause the picture to be underexposed.*

▲ *Moving the flash unit closer will allow you to acheive an exposure that is faithful to the subject.*

you have f/5.6. Then add the zero that you dropped earlier in the calculation. This gives you a guide number of 56.

Once you know the correct guide number for the film (or ISO equivalency) you're using, you can calculate flash-to-subject distance using the following formula:

Flash shooting distance =
Guide Number (GN) / f/stop (aperture)

For example, if your guide number is 56 (as per the above example) and your aperture is f/8 then your flash shooting distance should be 7 feet (2.13 metres). Once you have this base calculation you can determine where to position the flash based on your preferred exposure settings (as shown in illustration X).

Taking the above example a step further, let's say you want to shoot at f/11 rather than f/8. Where do you position the flash unit? Simple, using the above formula 56 (GN) divided by 11 (lens aperture) equals 5 feet (1.52 metres) (as shown in illustration Y).

What happens when you are unable to move the flash unit closer? In this situation you need to calculate the required lens aperture. You can do this by rearranging the formula above to become:

Lens aperture = Guide Number (GN) /
flash-to-subject distance

For example, let's say you are 16 feet (4.88 metres) from the subject and the guide number of your flash unit is 56. Using the new formula, 56 (GN) divided by 16 (flash-to-subject distance in feet) equals 3.5, giving you an aperture of f/3.5 (as shown in illustration Z).

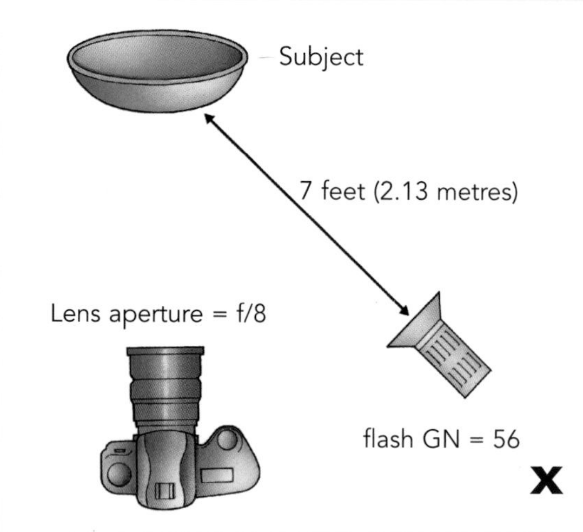

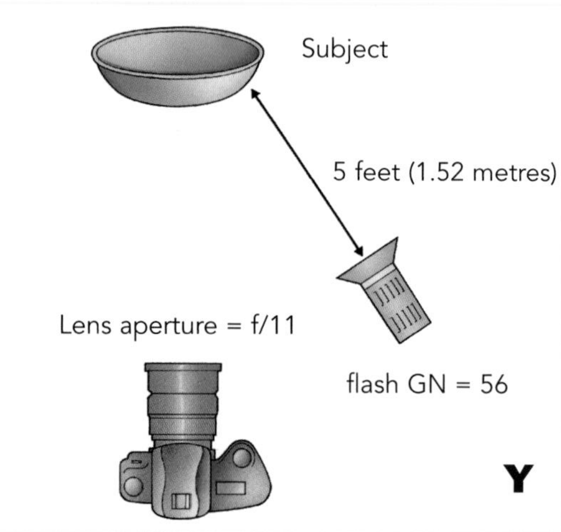

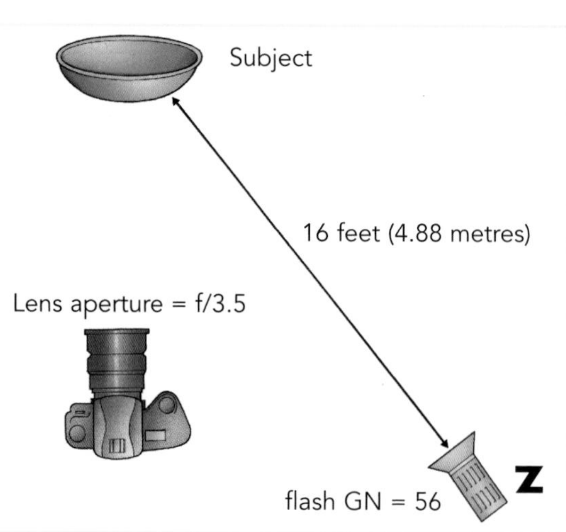

Exposure calculation for bounced flash

There may be occasions when you want to bounce flash off a wall or ceiling to soften the quality of light or make the light source larger. When you bounce flash using an automatic TTL flash unit then the same exposure calculations apply as above. This is because the camera is measuring the light entering through the lens and so will automatically take into account the extra distance the light is travelling and any absorption factor of the surface the flash is bounced off. Similarly, non-TTL automatic flash will work perfectly well so long as the sensor on the flash unit is pointed towards the subject.

However, if you are calculating flash exposure manually then you will need to change a couple of things. Firstly, you must calculate your exposure based on the total distance the flash has travelled. That is the distance from the flash unit to the reflective surface plus the distance from the surface to the subject. You will also need to compensate for light loss caused by absorption and scattering.

Exposure calculation for diffused flash

When you place a diffuser in front of your flash unit, the flash-to-subject distance won't change but you will lose some light through absorption. As with bounced flash, TTL-auto and non-TTL-auto flash units will automatically compensate for this loss of light. When calculating flash exposure manually, however, you will need to run some tests in order to measure the amount of light absorbed by the diffuser material (see box below).

For example, if your base lens aperture was f/16 and your correctly exposed test shot was taken with an aperture of f/11 then the difference between the two is one stop. Now, every time you use that particular diffuser you know to add one stop exposure compensation.

While it is possible to write an entire book on flash exposure, what I have discussed here should be sufficient for all but the most complicated of shooting situations. Like the question of exposure in general, it's not as complicated as it seems!

The absorption test

1. With your camera on a tripod and flash unit attached, compose your picture.
2. Take a picture without the diffuser attached to the flash unit, using the manual flash exposure calculations described earlier. Make a note of the exposure settings – this will be your base aperture.
3. Without moving the camera, attach the diffuser to the flash unit and take several more shots, opening the aperture by a 1/2 stop for each additional frame. Make a note of the aperture for each picture.
4. Ascertain which of the images is correctly exposed, refer to your notes and check the aperture used for that frame. The difference in stops between this aperture and the base aperture is the absorption value of the diffuser.

Post camera exposure

The focus of this book, and everything I have covered so far, is on achieving faithful exposures in-camera. And, I strongly urge you to aim for faithful exposures at the point of making the photograph.

◀ *Photography is, and has always been, a two part process - image capture and image processing. Today, the secrets of the darkroom, such as selective exposure, un-sharp mask and managing contrast are terms familiar to us all thanks to photo-enhancement software and computers.*

35mm camera, 24mm lens, Fuji Velvia, 1/10sec at f/32

The digital darkroom

There are times when the shooting conditions and the limitations of film/PS won't allow you to achieve the images you want. While I do not intend to write reams on this particular subject, I think it is important to at least cover the basics of what to do when the image coming out of the camera doesn't quite live up to expectations.

It's important to understand that I am not talking about manipulation. I strongly believe that 'rubbish in equals rubbish out' and that no amount of 'doctoring' will rescue a photograph that is poor in the first instance. What I am discussing is how to compensate for the limitations all photographers have to work with when the tools needed for in-camera adjustments are unavailable to you or the conditions imposed upon you are not suitable for making the kind of exposure that you want to.

Historically images would have been enhanced in the darkroom using selective printing techniques, such as those mastered by Ansel Adams and written about in his series of books The Camera, The Negative and The Print. This is a huge and varied subject, and there is a lot to be said for the 'hands on' enjoyment of the darkroom. However, the advent of modern technology and the expanding role of computers in photography means most post camera production is now made on the computer using specialized software, such as Adobe Photoshop.

It would require a complete book, and possibly several volumes, to cover the subject of software-based image enhancement in full. My aim here is to simply outline some of the basic functions available in such software programs.

Controlling contrast

As I have already discussed an image's contrast is measured by the grey scale. For an image to have a good tonal range (and therefore good contrast levels) it needs to make use of the full range of tones from black to white. When an image lacks tonal range it appears flat and uninteresting.

Using the 'levels' dialogue can alter the level of contrast in an image. This function uses a representative histogram to show the number of pixels at different brightness levels in an image and allows for the brightness of each pixel to be remapped so the darkest point corresponds to black and the brightest point to white. In a picture that lacks any real contrast, follow the steps in the box facing. By opening the 'levels' dialogue box in Photoshop you can see that the range of tones falls short of the full range available – 0 (black) to 255 (white).

Using the levels dialogue box

You can increase the level of contrast by re-mapping each pixel from the digital file (digital original or scanned film) following the steps outlined below.

1. First open the levels dialogue box – this can normally be found under the image tools list. You will see a histogram which serves as a visual guide of the image's 'key tones'.

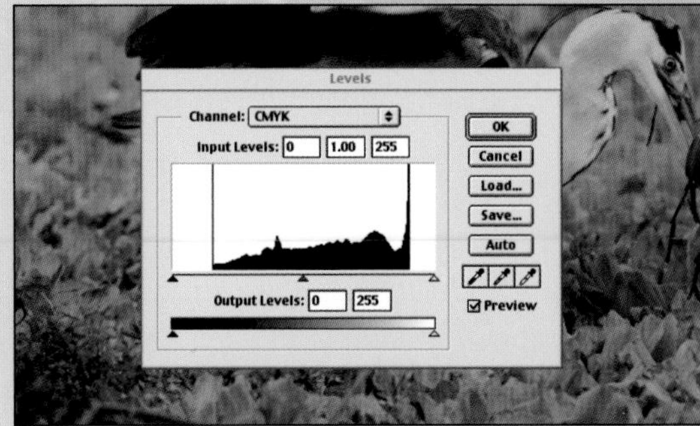

2. Re-map the shadows and highlights, by dragging the left-hand slider to the point where the histogram values cross zero at the bottom, and the right-hand slider to that point at the top.

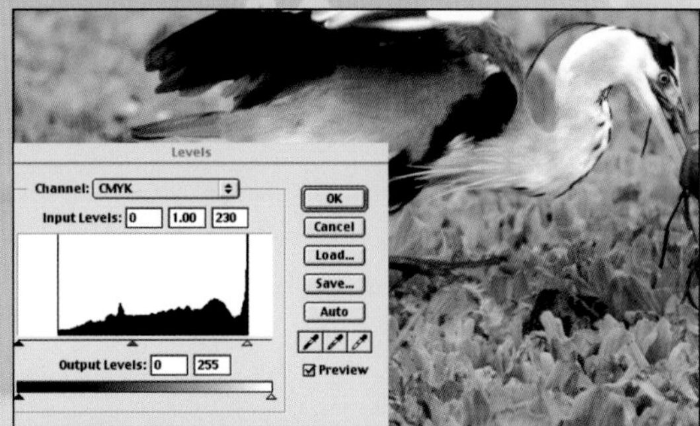

The result of this exercise is that the brightest pixels in the image are now mapped to white and the darkest pixels to black.

3. Finally, you can use the middle slider to change the level of the middle tones in the image without affecting the highlights or shadows to any great extent. You can experiment with this final phase until you get an image that you like.

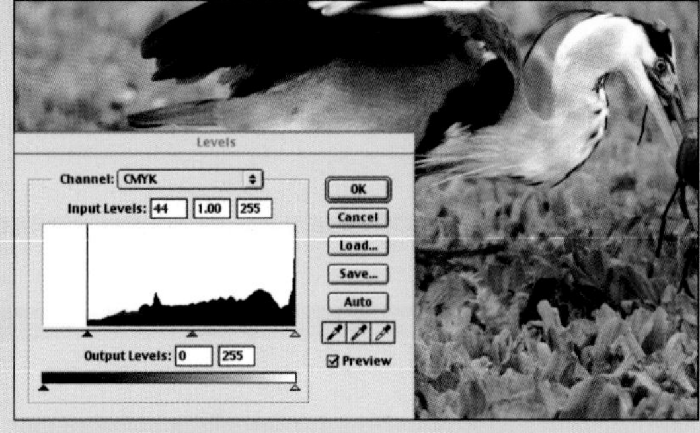

◀ *The image to the left now has a better tonal range than the original. This results in a stronger and more pleasing picture.*

Controlling colour

As well as adjusting the contrast of your image you can use the 'levels' dialogue to counteract colour problems caused by poor calibration, incorrect white balance or wrong film type.

Having defined the black and white points in an image you can tell the software exactly where in the picture these points are by using the black, grey and white eyedroppers. What this will now do is re-map the colour of the pixels.

You should be aware that without a properly calibrated computer monitor – which most people don't have – it is very difficult to make accurate changes using this tool.

It also saves you a lot of time fiddling around with the levels dialogue box, if you can work out what went wrong with the original exposure. This way you can correct a specific problem, rather than take a haphazard approach.

Finally, it is worth noting that colour adjustments can look very seductive when they are first made, only to look totally unrealistic when they are reviewed at a later date.

▶ *The resulting picture (bottom facing) has a better colour balance than the unadjusted image (top facing).*

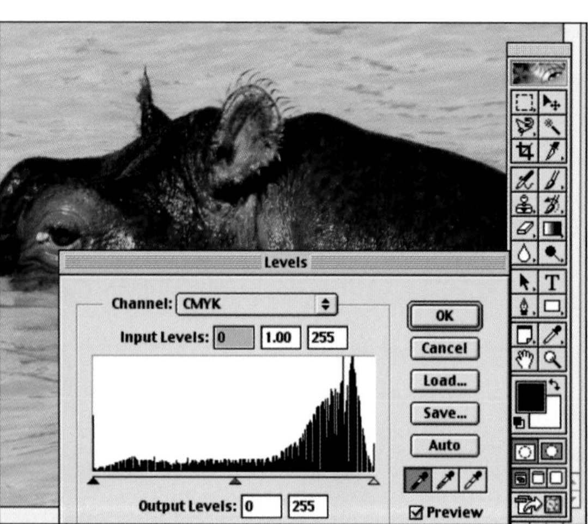

1. First, select the black eyedropper, move it to the darkest point of the image and click on that point.
2. Then, select the white eyedropper, move it to the brightest part of the image where detail is still visible and click on that point.
3. Finally, to define the grey point, select the grey eyedropper, drag it to a point on the image that should appear middle-tone grey and click on that point.

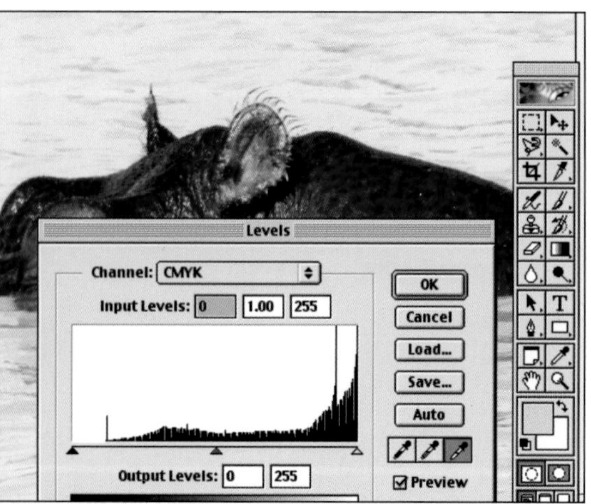

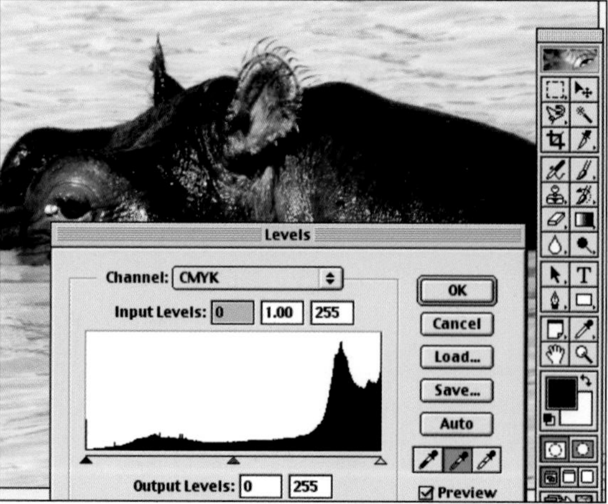

Selective exposure

The 'Levels' dialogue is an excellent application for adjusting the overall brightness of a scene. But what happens when you want to adjust very specific areas of an image?

Well, the old darkroom technique of 'dodging and burning' (giving different areas of the scene more or less exposure to lighten or darken them) is available via the computer.

Using the dodging tool will lighten selected areas of the scene while the burn tool will darken selected areas.

By using these tools selectively you can enhance the contrast of an image. You can also alter the size of the paintbrush so that you can be more precise.

In the example below some areas of the grassland have been 'dodged' to add highlights, while shadow areas underneath the wildebeest have been 'burnt in' to maintain the contrast. Compare the two images and the bottom image should have a much greater impact – because of the higher level of contrast – than the top image.

◀ *The image to the left is lacking contrast. The difference between the highlights and shadows is not great enough to give the photo impact.*

▼ *The image below has been 'dodged and burned' to enhance the final contrast.*

Magic wand

You can also use the 'magic wand' to brighten shadow areas or darken highlights in an image, without affecting the base exposure for the main image. Using the picture below as an example, the light shining on the left side of the lion's face is overexposed compared with the main image. By selecting the magic wand function in Photoshop and clicking on the affected area you can use the 'levels curves' tool to darken the highlights.

▶ The light falling on the left-hand side of the lion has overexposed this part of the image. The base exposure is fine (as you can see from the rest of the image), so the 'magic wand' is the tool to use.

◀ The image of the lion now has a more even exposure – compare the left-hand side of the image to the image above. This has enhanced the impact of the image as a whole.

Chapter 8

Using exposure to create evocative images

What I have described so far in the book is the process for calculating technically accurate exposures. And you could be forgiven for going through your photographic life never deviating from these rules – probably winning many competitions along the way. The importance of photographic rules, however, is not that you stick to them with an insipid rigidity, but that they provide you with a starting point – a base calculation – from which you can decide how you want the scene to appear in the final image.

◀ *Through precise control of a camera's exposure settings you can make even the most mundane of subjects appear to shine with visual energy.*

35mm camera, 800mm lens, 1/15sec at f/5.6

At the beginning of this book I described how what you should be striving for in your photography is not simply correct exposure but faithful exposure – exposures that help record the subject as you saw it at that very moment in time. Exposures that are technically correct may not achieve this, and how you apply your imagination to exposure settings goes a long way to defining your photographic signature.

The following case studies illustrate how I took control from the camera to set exposures that deviated from the meter's recommended settings in order to create images that mirrored faithfully the emotions I felt at the time. Each case study describes the effects I set out to achieve, how I determine my exposure values and how I manipulated the camera to make it produce the results that I had pre-visualized.

What each case study effectively illustrates is the premise with which I started this book: that there is no such thing as correct exposures, simply faithful ones.

Case Study - 1

People 1

In glamour photography there is no doubt that less is sometimes more. So, when taking this picture, my aim was to create an image of simplicity and to isolate the model from her surroundings. Sometimes this can be achieved by using depth of field to blur any foreground or background detail. On this occasion, however, I have used light to achieve the same effect – in fact, too much light.

This particular image – and this style of image – is created by grossly overexposing the background. Two studio flash units were used to light the model (one unit as the main light and a second unit to lift the shadows created by the first light), and a third flash unit was used to light the background. I took a meter reading from the model's face and used this as my base exposure setting. I then increased the power of the third (background) light to give an EV four times higher, which has helped to create the overexposed, washed-out background.

The effect used here isolates the model and focuses all your attention where I want it to be – which is on her.

Case Study - 2

People 2

With this image I have continued the theme of simplicity and used contrast – a balance of highlights and shadows – to delineate form. The key to creating a photograph like this is to ensure that the subject's brightness range (SBR) is beyond the latitude of the film or photo-sensor being used, thereby creating a range of tones from pure, featureless black to pure, featureless white (or in this case red, where a red gel has been placed over the main light source).

I used two studio flash units to make this picture. A direct, point light source covered with a red filter and positioned to the right of the model was used as the main light and creates the bright highlights and hard shadows. A second flash unit was used from behind the left of the model to soften the shadows on the back and lighten the background, which would otherwise have merged in with the model giving no separation. I then took a meter reading of the highlights on the model's right cheek and forehead, followed by a meter reading of the shadow area on the left side of her face. Finally, I took a reading from the very dark shadows of the area between her two arms.

These three readings gave me an SBR of over nine stops, which is outside the latitude of the photo-sensor I was using and so I set an exposure in the middle of the two extremes, ensuring the high level of contrast I was after. The red filter was added to heighten the impact of the photograph.

Case Study - 3

Cities I

You can have great fun photographing cities, particularly in low-light and night conditions – the mixture of natural and artificial light creating an intriguing juxtaposition. For this first image I used a much-practised technique of zooming out with the lens during a long-time exposure. This technique creates the streaks of light from the artificial street lamps and office lights, while the natural light produces a double image of the city's skyscrapers and office blocks.

It is a simple technique to replicate: attach a zoom lens with a relatively broad range, (e.g. 28mm–100mm) to your camera and attach the camera to a sturdy tripod. Then, set an exposure of at least three seconds. (If your shutter speed is slower than three seconds then close down the lens aperture and reduce the shutter speed by an equal and opposite amount.) After you have triggered the shutter, zoom the lens out from its longest focal length to its shortest. Do this evenly over the course of the exposure using gentle movements to minimize camera shake.

The photograph you will create will be an unusual composition of lighting effects, which you may or may not appreciate. It never hurts to experiment though!

Case Study - 4

Cities 2

This second image of a cityscape is far more traditional than the first and is equally as intriguing in its design. The main feature of this photograph is its sense of place, created by the wide angle of view and also by the inclusion of Mount Rainier in the background. The mountain is important to the composition and I needed a large depth of field to render it sharp – even though it is somewhat obscured by the summer haze.

To calculate the exposure I took a meter reading from the sky and applied a plus one stop exposure compensation, giving me an EV of 13. I needed a small aperture to maximize the depth of field and chose f/11, which left me with a shutter speed of 1/60. Because of the high level of haze and because I wanted to give the picture depth I also set the contrast setting on my digital SLR to high, which helps to accentuate the highlights and shadow areas of the scene.

The resulting photograph is an atmospheric portrait of this city and its relationship with the environment around it, created by the controlled and deliberate use of lens aperture and shutter speed mechanics.

Case Study - 5

Landscape

What we see with two eyes and a constantly changing aperture (our pupils) is quite different to what the camera sees with a single lens and a fixed aperture. This can make taking good landscape photographs, and indeed any other subject, quite difficult. The problem tends to come when recreating depth in a two-dimensional medium such as a photographic print.

Depth, or at least the perception of depth is depicted in photographs by contrast – highlights and shadows – and photographic exposure is really all about your ability to balance contrast within the latitude of the film or photo-sensor. The direction of light plays a key role here, as with this picture taken in Alaska. Light falling on a subject from a low angle, such as you'd expect to see at sunrise and sunset, casts hard, long shadows that accentuate form.

Your job, then, as the photographer is to capture these areas of highlight and shadow faithfully. For this photograph I used the flat top of the mountain formation as my medium tone and took a spot meter reading. I then took two further readings, one from the sky and one from the trees in the foreground to assess the SBR. Because the sky was quite bright I added a NDG filter of two stops' strength to help even the tones and used my initial meter reading to set the exposure.

Without the right balance of highlights and shadows this image would lose much of its visual impact and again demonstrates the key role that exposure plays in creating compelling pictures.

Case Study - 6

Wildlife I

I saw this solitary baboon looking contemplative at the side of a waterhole in the Kruger National Park in South Africa. It was late evening, around sunset, and the light was tinged with a beautiful warm glow. In making this image, rather than photographing a simple portrait of the animal, I wanted to capture the mood the animal was in, illustrated in great depth by its eyes.

I took a meter reading with the TTL meter in spot mode, which gave me my exposure value. Interpreting this information, knowing that the angle of coverage of the light meter was too wide for my purposes, had I shot at the given exposure value the eyes would have been underexposed, losing their detail and prominence.

So, in order to retain the high level of detail and place the emphasis of the picture on the eyes of the baboon, I reduced the exposure by 1⅓ stops by altering the shutter speed and thereby retaining control over depth of field. This rendered most of the scene slightly out of focus but kept the eyes sharp. This heightened the emphasis I wanted to place on them.

Case Study - 7

Wildlife 2

One of the great difficulties of wildlife photography is that many of my subjects are most active at night. This is not because I have a hankering to photograph nocturnal creatures, simply a nuance of nature herself.

On a night drive through a private game reserve in the Mpumalanga region of South Africa we came across a pride of lions – three lionesses, one male and three sprightly cubs. Observing their behaviour it became obvious that food was high on their agenda and they had picked up the scent of nearby prey.

In making this picture it was this activity I wanted to capture. The difficulty was in getting enough light to expose any image at all. Even with my fastest telephoto lens (300mm f/2.8) the light was too dim to record an acceptable image. Because I was using a digital camera I first set the ISO equivalency to 1,600, increasing the photo-sensors' sensitivity to light and allowing me a shutter speed just fast enough to ensure a sharp image. Then, I took a meter reading using the TTL meter in spot mode, which gave me an EV of 4. Lighting was provided by a hand-held spotlight, which concentrates a powerful beam of light over a small area. The effect is very similar to direct sunlight and I knew that this would fool the camera into overexposing the image at the point of concentration. Normally, I would have stopped down by around 1½ stops. However, because I knew the lioness to be one stop brighter than middle tone I anticipated the TTL reading to be one stop underexposed. I added the additional 1/2 stop change to achieve an exposure that emphasizes the behaviour of the animal, which was the image I imagined.

Case Study - 8

Birds I

Observing this bird in a remote region of South Africa I was fascinated by its perpetual movement. It simply never stood still, constantly bobbing along the shore probing for sustenance. A typical record shot of this bird would have rendered it pin sharp and technically perfectly exposed. But I wasn't interested in records and wanted a picture that captured the dynamic nature of this avian character. Question was, how to go about it?

If I had exposed for the bird itself the emphasis of the picture would have been placed on the species and not on the motion I was trying to portray. Because there is enough information contained within the form of the bird to tell you its species I decided on a silhouette, removing all detail from the body and thereby shifting the emphasis away from the subject itself. To achieve this I took a meter reading from the background and opened up one stop to render it brighter than middle tone, as it appeared to the naked eye. If I had wanted to freeze the action then I would have used a fast shutter speed (1/125sec or faster). However, on this occasion purposely I wanted to capture the sense of motion and so set a slower shutter speed (1/15sec) that created the edge of blur that gives the photograph its emotion.

This image is another example of how by controlling the settings of the camera you can make a photograph that communicates mood and emotion, rather than plain and simple record shots.

Case Study - 9

Wildlife 3

Again, this image is all about using the camera's exposure controls to create the desired effect. The image was taken from a micro-light aircraft above the Kruger National Park in South Africa. Before I took off I had a clear picture in my mind of the photograph I wanted to make, placing an emphasis not simply on motion but also on speed.

Two things help to capture that effect. One is the movement of the elephants as they run through the brush; the other is the speed of the micro-light as it cuts through the air. The challenge here was to capture both to a degree where they complemented each other.

Had I wanted to freeze the motion then I would have used a fast shutter speed and panned the camera to counter the forward motion of the aircraft, which would have rendered the elephants sharp but not achieved the effect I wanted. So, I chose a slow shutter speed (1/30sec) and held the camera steady. This created the soft blur around the edges of the elephants together with the streaks in the ground that can clearly be seen, particularly in the top right corner. Together they achieve a sense of celerity that mimics perfectly the scene I witnessed from my seat above the ground.

Case Study - 10

Nature I

This picture is a study in how to make grass look interesting! Once again, you will notice that motion plays a particular role in the message that this image communicates. Above and beyond motion, however, what really makes this picture work is the way in which motion and light interact.

What I wanted to emphasize in this scene was the way that the early morning sunlight was catching the grass stalks as they stirred in the breeze, creating a glitter-like effect across the whole scene.

The challenge was to get the right combination of lens aperture and shutter speed because I wanted a slow shutter speed to create the illusion of motion and a large lens aperture for minimal depth of field, so enhancing the abstract nature of the picture and placing the emphasis on the splashes of bright light and away from the grass stalks themselves. However, because it was a relatively bright day already, to get the right combination I needed a little extra help. To darken the overall brightness of the scene I used a neutral density filter (non-graduated), which allowed me to reduce the shutter speed by two stops (to 1/15sec), slow enough to create the blur I wanted.

Once again, what you see here is a photograph that communicates much more than simply the identity of the subject and illustrates how an understanding of exposure and effective use of the camera's exposure controls can evoke pictures within pictures.

Case Study - 11

Birds 2

OK, a more traditional picture to consider. The main challenge in calculating exposure when photographing birds in flight is that the surface you are photographing, i.e. the underside of the bird, is often shaded from the main light source, the sun. Now, if you were close enough then fill-in flash would work well here. Unfortunately, the bird is often far overhead and out of range of the average flash unit. Spot metering would work, too, if you have enough time and control over the metering brackets to keep the bird within the scope of the spot meter – not an easy task! So, what to do?

Actually, with this picture, the answer is quite simple. The image was taken around about late morning on a bright clear day – perfect for the 'sunny f/16' rule. The most important feature of the bird to get right was the eye, which, as you can see from the highlight, is facing towards the sun. I was shooting with ISO 100 film and so set my exposure to an appropriate combination, in this instance 1/800sec at f/5.6, using the fast shutter speed to freeze the action.

(The exposure setting was calculated by working down from the 'sunny f/16' rule: f/16 at 1/100sec, f/11 at 1/200sec, f/8 at 1/400sec and, finally, f/5.6 at 1/800sec.)

I made no further adjustments and concentrated on getting an effective composition. Reverting to the 'sunny f/16' rule is a leap of faith for many photographers. But, as you can see quite clearly from this image, sometimes we can overcomplicate the technical aspects of photography when often the simple things work best.

Case Study - 12

Wildlife 4

Sorry, I couldn't resist another 'motion' shot to round things off. I had been sitting on the banks of this pan in South Africa's Mkuze Game Reserve for the best part of a day, watching this pod of hippos laze their time away. As the afternoon drew on the light changed to a beautiful, warm yellow and was catching the bulbous faces of the hippos nearest where I sat.

The thing about hippos is they don't do very much. But when they decide to move, even only slightly, they create all sorts of havoc: mud and water flying everywhere with every crashing action. And, it was this maelstrom of activity I wanted to photograph and the secret to my success was getting the exposure settings just right.

The sunlight was catching perfectly the splashes of water thrown by the movement of the hippos and this is what I wanted to expose for. Because they were so small I wanted to exaggerate the prominence in the scene and opted for a slow shutter speed that would create the curling streaks as they fell away from the yawning hippo towards the ground.

I used my TTL spot meter to take a reading from the brightest part of the hippo's skin. Because I knew the tone to be far brighter than middle tone I then opened up the given reading by 1½ stops to compensate and set a slow shutter speed of 1/10sec.

This image, like the others depicted in this section of the book, gives a much greater sense of the overall emotion within this scene, above and beyond a simple portrait or record shot. It is full of action and emotion and, like it or loathe it, achieves an image that is set apart from contemporary views.

Glossary

18% grey – The middle point between a films' ability to read detail in featureless black and featureless white.

81 series filter – A filter type that produces a warm colour cast by reducing the level of blue light reaching the film. They can also correct cold colour casts.

Absorption – The process by which incident light is partially absorbed by the subject it is falling on.

Accessory shoe – A fitting on top of a camera which allows accessories to be attached.

Adams, Ansel – American landscape photographer and pioneer of the zone system.

Adobe Photoshop – A widely used image manipulation program.

AE – see Automatic exposure.

AF – see Autofocus.

Ambient light – The available light, without intervention from the photographer, by which to take photographs.

Angle of incidence – The angle between the incident light falling on the light source and the reflected light entering the camera lens.

Angle of view – The area of a scene that a lens takes in. A wide-angle lens, such as 28mm, has a wide angle of view. A telephoto lens, such as 300mm, has a narrow angle of view.

Aperture – The hole or opening formed by the metal leaf diaphragm inside the lens or the opening in a camera lens through which light passes to expose the film. The size of the aperture is denoted by f/numbers.

Aperture priority – An exposure mode on an automatic camera where the photographer sets the aperture and the camera sets the shutter speed for correct exposure. If the aperture is changed, or the light level changes, the shutter speed changes automatically.

Aperture ring – A ring, located on the lens barrel, which is linked mechanically to the diaphragm to control the size of the aperture.

Artificial light – Light from a man-made source, such as a flash unit, household bulb, fluorescent tube or strobe light.

Artificial light film – Colour film used for balancing the colour cast caused by tungsten artificial light.

ASA – American Standards Association. Group that determined the numerical ratings of speed for US-manufactured photo-sensitive products such as camera film. ISO ratings are now more commonly used.

Autoexposure bracketing – A setting on the camera whereby the camera will automatically adjust the initial exposure setting by a pre-defined amount (usually around 1/3 or 1/2 stop) for one, two or more subsequent exposures of the same scene.

Autofocus (AF) – System by which the focusing function is automatically controlled by the camera. Different manufacturers use different systems and you should check your manual for details.

Automatic camera – A camera with a built-in exposure meter that automatically adjusts the lens opening, shutter speed, or both, for the correct exposure.

Automatic exposure (AE) – The setting on a camera whereby the camera selects the appropriate lens aperture/shutter speed combination for a correct exposure, given the meter readings it has taken.

Available light – Light occurring naturally in a scene. As opposed to artificial light.

Backlighting – Light coming from the far side of the subject, towards the camera lens.

Balanced fill-in flash – A type of TTL auto flash operation which uses the camera's exposure meter to control ambient light exposure settings, integrated with flash exposure control.

Barn doors – An accessory used to concentrate the light from studio flash units.

Bellows – The folding portion in some cameras that connects the lens to the camera body. Also a camera accessory that, when inserted between the lens and camera body, extends the lens-to-film distance for close focusing or macro photography.

Blur – An unsharp image or image area caused by subject or camera movement, or incorrect or selective focusing.

Bounced flash – The process of using a wall or ceiling to bounce light from a flash unit onto the subject. This is used to 'soften' shadows.

Bracketing – The process of exposing a series of frames of the same subject or scene at different exposure settings.

Bulb setting – A shutter-speed setting on an adjustable camera that allows for timed exposures. When set on Bulb, the shutter will stay open as long as the shutter release button remains depressed. This is often used for especially long exposures.

Burning-in – A darkroom technique that gives additional exposure to part of the image projected on an enlarger easel to make that area of the print darker. This can also be done digitally, by using image manipulation software such as Adobe Photoshop.

Cable release – Flexible cable used to fire the shutter remotely.

Calibration – Determining the accuracy of photographic equipment in order to provide base readings from which accurate measurements can be made.

Camera shake – Movement of camera caused by an unsteady hold or support. This can lead, particularly at slower shutter speeds, to a blurred image on the film.

Capacitor – An electrical component of a flash which controls its output.

Cast – Abnormal colouring of an image produced by departure from recommended exposure or processing conditions with a transparency film, or when making a colour print.

CCD (charge-coupled device) – A microchip made up of light-sensitive cells and used in digital cameras for recording images.

Centre-weighted metering – A type of metering system that apportions a high level of the exposure calculation on the amount of light falling at the centre of the picture space. This is suitable for portraits or scenes where subjects fill the centre of the frame.

Close-up – A picture taken with the subject close to the camera.

Close-up lens – A lens attachment placed in front of a camera lens to permit taking pictures at a closer distance than the camera lens alone will allow.

CMOS (complementary metal oxide semi-conductor) – A microchip made up of light-sensitive cells and used in digital cameras for recording images.

Cold colours – Colours at the blue end of the visible spectrum.

Colour correction filters – Filters that are used to correct colour casts.

Colour temperature – Description of the colour of a light source by comparing it with the colour of light emitted by a theoretical perfect radiator at a particular temperature expressed in Kelvins (K).

Composition – The arrangement of the design elements within the picture space.

Contrast – The range of difference between the highlight and shadow areas of a negative, print, slide or digital image.

Contrast filters – Filters used in black and white photography to introduce contrast between two different colours that would normally record as a similar shade of grey.

Critical aperture – The aperture setting at which a lens performs the best. In other words an aperture which balances quality lost by diffraction at narrow apertures and quality lost by lens aberrations at wide apertures.

Cropping – Printing only part of the available image from the negative, slide or digital file, usually to improve composition.

Daylight colour film – Colour film intended for use with light sources with a colour temperature of approximately 5400K. For example daylight.

Dedicated – An accessory that is designed for use with a specific camera or camera range.

Depth of field – The zone of acceptable sharpness in front of and behind the subject on which the lens is focused.

Diaphragm – The adjustable aperture of a lens.

Diffuse lighting – Lighting that is low or moderate in contrast, such as that which occurs on an overcast day.

Dodging – Holding back the image-forming light from a part of the image projected on an enlarger easel during part of the exposure to make that area of the print lighter.

Down-rating – Applied to film speed, where the manufacturer's set film speed, measured in ISO, is manually reduced and the film is exposed at a slower film speed.

DX (digital index) – Coding on the film cartridges used to transmit information in relation to film speed, the length of film and the exposure latitude to the camera.

EV (exposure value) – A measurement of light given by an exposure meter that enables exposure settings to be derived.

Exposure – The quantity of light allowed to act on a photographic material.

Exposure compensation – A level of adjustment given (generally) to autoexposure settings that adjusts for known inaccuracies in the camera's automatically chosen exposure settings.

Exposure latitude – The range of exposures from underexposure to overexposure that will produce acceptable pictures from a specific film.

Exposure meter – An instrument with a light-sensitive cell that measures the light reflected from or falling on a subject, used as an aid for selecting the exposure setting.

Extension bellows – Device used to provide the additional separation between lens and film required for close-up photography.

Extension tubes – Metal tubes used to obtain the additional separation between lens and film for close-up photography.

f/numbers – A series of numbers on the lens aperture ring and/or the camera's LCD panel that indicate the size of the lens' aperture.

f/stops – A fraction that indicates the actual diameter of the aperture: the "f" represents the lens focal length, the slash means "divided by", and the word "stop" is a particular f-number.

Fill-in flash – Method of flash photography that combines flash illumination and ambient light, but does not balance these two types of illumination. See also Balanced fill-in flash.

Film – A photographic emulsion coated on a flexible, transparent base that records light.

Film latitude – The range, measured in f/stops, between highlight and shadow that a film can record detail.

Film plane – The plane in which the film lies.

Film speed – The sensitivity of a given film to light, measured in ISO.

Filter – A piece of coloured glass, or other transparent material, used over the lens to emphasize, eliminate, or change the colour or density of the entire scene or certain areas within a scene.

Flare – Non-image-forming light present in the lens barrel which produces coloured shapes or a loss of contrast in the final image.

Flash – A form of artificial light generated by the full or partial discharge of a capacitor.

Flash synchronization – The synchronization of flash duration and shutter speed.

Flat lighting – Lighting that produces very little contrast and minimal shadow.

Focal length – The distance between the film and the optical centre of the lens when the lens is focused on infinity, measured in millimetres.

Focus – Adjustment of the distance setting on a lens to define the subject sharply. Generally, the act of adjusting a lens to produce a sharp image.

Front lighting – Light shining on the surface of the subject facing the camera. This can produce dull lifeless photos although is good for picking out surface detail.

Grain – Minute metallic silver deposit, forming in quantity the photographic image on film.

Graininess – The sand-like or granular appearance of a negative, print, or slide. Graininess generally becomes more pronounced with faster film and the degree of enlargement makes it more noticeable.

Grey card – A grey card that reflects 18% of the light falling on it, representative of a middle-toned subject.

Guide number – A figure that denotes the maximum power of a flash unit as a distance. It is normally given in metres or feet when used with ISO 100 film.

High contrast – A wide range of density in a slide, print, negative or digital file.

Highlights – Very bright part of an image or object that is generally lacking in any detail.

Hotshoe – An accessory shoe with electrical contacts allowing synchronization between the camera and accessory.

Hot-spot – An un-wished for concentration of light on a subject. This is a problem common to flash photography.

Incident light – Light falling on a surface.

Incident light meters – Hand-held light meters used for measuring light falling on a surface

ISO – The international standard for representing film sensitivity. The emulsion speed (sensitivity) of the film as determined by the standards of the International Standards Organization.

Kelvin (K) – A scale used to measure temperature of colour.

Landscape-format – A picture format where the frame is wider than it is tall.

Large-format – A term referring to a negative or transparency with a size of 5" x 4" or greater.

LCD (liquid crystal display) panel – A screen on a camera that provides information in the form of alphanumeric characters and symbols. Often used to display exposure settings, frame count, ISO rating, etc.

Lens – One or more pieces of optical glass, or similar material, designed to collect and focus rays of light to form a sharp image.

Lens barrel – The structure within which the optical elements of a lens are held.

Lens hood – Device used to prevent non-image-forming light from entering the lens barrel and causing flare.

Lens speed – The largest lens opening (smallest f/number) at which a lens can be set.

Light meter – See Exposure meter.

Macro Lens – A lens that provides continuous focusing from infinity to extreme close-ups, often to a reproduction ratio of 1:1 or 'life-size' (true macro), or sometimes larger.

Middle tone – A tone of grey or any other colour that reflects 18% of the light falling on it.

Motor drive – An automatic winding mechanism that advances or rewinds film.

Multi-segment metering – An exposure metering system using a number of variable sized and positioned segments in conjunction with an in-camera computer to detect brightness levels and provide an exposure value based on pre-defined precedents.

Negative film – A type of film which is used to produce prints.

Neutral density (ND) – A filter that reduces light entering the lens without changing the colour.

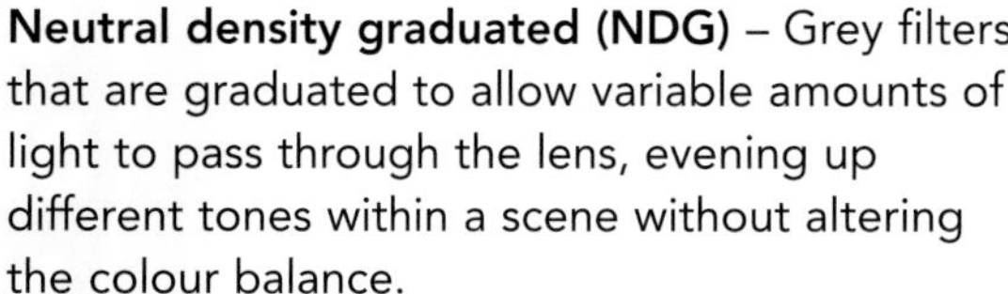

Neutral density graduated (NDG) – Grey filters that are graduated to allow variable amounts of light to pass through the lens, evening up different tones within a scene without altering the colour balance.

Noise – The digital equivalent of graininess, caused by stray electrical signals.

Normal lens – A lens that makes the image in a photograph appear in perspective similar to that of the original scene as seen by the human eye (approximately 45°).

Opening up – Increasing the size of the aperture of the lens to allow more light to hit the film or photo-sensor.

Optical axis – A theoretical line passing through the centre of a lens from front to back

Overexposure – A condition in which too much light reaches the film or PS, producing a dense negative or a very bright/light print or slide. Detail is lost in the highlights.

PC – Personal computer.

Pentaprism – A five-sided prism that is used in SLR cameras to give a correctly oriented image in the viewfinder.

Photo-sensor (PS) – The device that records light in a digital camera.

Polarizing filter – A filter that transmits light travelling in one plane while absorbing light travelling in other planes. When placed in front of a camera lens, it can eliminate undesirable reflections from a subject such as water, glass, or other objects with a shiny surface. Also used to saturate colours (e.g. to make blue skies darker).

Polarized light – Light waves vibrating in one plane only as opposed to the multi-directional vibrations of normal rays. This occurs when light is reflected off certain surfaces.

Portrait-format – A picture format where the frame is taller than it is wide.

Program exposure – An exposure mode on an automatic camera that automatically sets both the aperture and the shutter speed for proper exposure.

Pull processing – Reducing the development time of a film to reduce its effective speed.

Push processing – Increasing the development time of a film to increase its effective speed (ISO rating). Often used in low-light situations.

Reciprocity law – A change in one exposure setting can be compensated for by an equal and corresponding change in the other. For example, the exposure settings of 1/125sec at f/8 produce exactly the same amount of light falling on the film/PS as 1/60sec at f/11.

Reciprocity law failure – At shutter speeds in excess of one second the law of reciprocity begins to fail because the sensitivity of film reduces over time. This affects different films to different extents.

Reflectance value – The amount of light, given as a percentage, that is reflected by the surface of an object.

Reflected light – Light reflected from the surface of a subject.

Reflected light meter – A light meter measuring light reflected from, rather than light falling on, the surface of a subject.

Sensitivity – Expression of the nature of a photographic emulsion's response to light. Can be concerned with degree of sensitivity as expressed by film speed or response to light of various colours, (spectral sensitivity).

Shutter – A curtain, plate, or some other movable cover in a camera that controls the time during which light reaches the film.

Shutter priority – An exposure mode on an automatic camera that lets you select the desired shutter speed; the camera sets the aperture for correct exposure. If you change the shutter speed, or the light level changes, the camera adjusts the aperture automatically.

Shutter speed – The length of time that the shutter is open. Measured in seconds or fractions of a second.

Side lighting – Light striking the subject from the side, relative to the position of the camera.

Silhouette – An extreme example of a backlit image in which all surface detail is lost.

Single lens reflex (SLR) – A type of camera that allows you to see through the camera's lens as you look in the camera's viewfinder. Other camera functions may also operate through the camera's lens.

Snoot – A circular attachment for studio flash units that creates a small circle of light.

Softbox – An attachment that softens the light of a studio flash unit.

Spot metering – A metering mode that takes a light reading from a very small portion of the scene, often as little as 1°.

Stop – The unit of measurement of light commonly used in photography.

Stopping down – Changing the lens aperture to a smaller opening. For example, from f/8 to f/11. Generally, can be used to mean any reduction in exposure either in aperture of shutter speed.

Subject brightness range (SBR) – The exposure range between the lightest portion of a scene and the darkest.

Telephoto lens – A lens with a narrow angle of view often giving the appearance of small subjects appearing larger in the picture space.

Through-the-lens (TTL) metering – A meter built into the camera that determines exposure for the scene by reading light that passes through the lens during picture taking.

Time exposure – A comparatively long exposure made in seconds or minutes.

Tungsten light film – Colour film that gives a correct colour balance under tungsten lighting.

Ultraviolet (UV) – Part of the electro-magnetic spectrum. Ulraviolet consists of wavelengths shorter than light and is therefore invisible to the human eye but can be recorded by photo-sensitive material.

Umbrella – A studio flash attachment that spreads the light.

Underexposure – A condition in which too little light reaches the film, producing a thin negative, a dark slide, or a muddy-looking print or digital file. There is too much detail lost in the areas of shadow in the exposure.

Up-rating – Applied to film speed, where the manufacturers set film speed, measured in ISO, is manually increased and the film is exposed at a faster film speed (e.g. an ISO 200 film can be up-rated to an ISO 400 film).

Vignetting – The intentional or unintentional darkening of the corners of an image. This is caused either by partially obscuring the lens or can be created in the darkroom.

Warm colours – Colours at the red end of the visible spectrum.

Wide-angle lens – A lens that has a shorter focal length and a wider field of view (includes more subject area) than a normal lens.

Zone system – A system for calculating exposure designed by Ansel Adams.

Zoom lens – A lens with a variable focal length.

About the author

Chris Weston is a full-time photographer and photojournalist. Chris has photographed elusive animals in some of the most hostile regions of the world and has the proven ability to get the right image time after time.

A regular contributor to numerous magazines and the author of several books, Chris also runs various photographic workshops both in the UK and abroad, through his own company Natural Photographic. He is also a co-founder of the Association of Professional Nature Photographers.

Index

E

F

G

H

I

K

L

M

N

photographers' pip institute press

TITLES AVAILABLE FROM
THE PHOTOGRAPHERS' INSTITUTE PRESS

The Photographers' Institute Press, PIP, is an exciting name in photography publishing. When you see this name on the spine of a book, you will be sure that the author is an experienced photographer and the content is of the highest standard, both technically and visually. Formed as a mark of quality, the Photographers' Institute Press covers the full range of photographic interests, from expanded camera guides to exposure techniques and landscape.

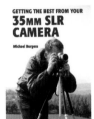

Animal Photographs: A Practical Guide
Robert Maier
ISBN 1 86108 303 3

Approaching Photography Paul Hill
ISBN 1 86108 323 8

Bird Photography: A Global Site Guide
David Tipling
ISBN 1 86108 302 5

Digital SLR Masterclass Andy Rouse
ISBN 1 86108 358 0

Garden Photography: A Professional Guide
Tony Cooper
ISBN 1 86108 392 0

Getting the Best from Your 35mm SLR Camera Michael Burgess
ISBN 1 86108 347 5

How to Photograph Dogs Nick Ridley
ISBN 1 86108 332 7

Photographers' Guide to Web Publishing
Charles Saunders
ISBN 1 86108 352 1

Photographing Changing Light: A Guide for Landscape Photographers
Ken Scott
ISBN 1 86108 380 7

Photographing Flowers Sue Bishop
ISBN 1 86108 366 1

Photographing People Roderick Macmillan
ISBN 1 86108 313 0

Photographing Water in the Landscape
David Tarn
ISBN 1 86108 396 3

The Photographic Guide to Exposure
Chris Weston
ISBN 1 86108 387 4

The PIP Expanded Guide to the: Nikon F5
Chris Weston
ISBN 1 86108 382 3

The PIP Expanded Guide to the: Nikon F80/N80 Matthew Dennis
ISBN 1 86108 348 3

The PIP Expanded Guide to the: Canon EOS 300/Rebel 2000 Matthew Dennis
ISBN 1 86108 338 6

Travel Photography: An Essential Guide
Rob Flemming
ISBN 1 86108 362 9

The list represents a selection of titles currently published or scheduled to be published.

All are available direct from the Publishers or through bookshops and specialist retailers.

To place an order, or to obtain a complete catalogue, contact:

Photographers' Institute Press,
Castle Place,
166 High Street, Lewes,
East Sussex BN7 1XU
United Kingdom

Tel: 01273 488005
Fax: 01273 402866
E-mail: pubs@thegmcgroup.com

Orders by credit card are accepted

Made in the USA
Columbia, SC
27 April 2021

Freedom Pony is Adopted was written as I earnestly wanted to communicate with children, all children, the deep love of the Father and the family we have in the Church. There is much more to say regarding healing, faith, and joy in our adoption! Please keep this conversation going with your local church as you walk through the hope of your salvation and commitment to your brothers and sisters in Christ.

There's a reason God leaves us on earth after we are adopted into His family: to tell others about this amazing, saving grace through our Lord. This mission is a reality which cannot be journeyed passively: we must be attentive, and pray for clear mindedness. The Father has powerfully provided weapons to bring to battle on a daily basis... weapons of strength and light which defeat fear and darkness! This little story, *The Mission*, is simplistic in its description of weapons, while the living Bible teaches all we need to know about warfare. His Word gives us instruction about guarding our hearts and minds, the use of words, light versus darkness, the armor of God, and more. Each time, "The weapons we fight with are not the weapons of the world. On the contrary, they have divine power to demolish strongholds", (2 Corinthians 10:4, NIV). This story was written in hopes to reveal how "contrary" these weapons are, compared to the artillery and strategy of the world, the enemy, and our own natural tendencies. My prayer is that our children will know they are not only equipped to defend, but to go on offense for the souls of the world by the power of the Holy Spirit.

"I have come as a light to shine in this dark world, so that all who put their trust in me will no

longer remain in the dark." -Jesus Christ

John 12:46

“Three things will last forever—faith, hope, and love—and the greatest of these is love.”

1 Corinthians 13:13

"Love for man and love for Christ!
Love that's shown through sacrifice!
Love for friends and family!
Love for you and love for me!
Love that is so strong and true,
I choose to love my enemies too!"

Freedom Ponies cheered her on!
Her faith and love were growing strong!
But there was one more gift to give.
Her Wings of Hope needed to live.
The wings were light but very large,
As Sister Pony sang this charge:
"Hope that hardships help us grow,
And God has plans that I don't know.
Hope that fills my soul and mind,
Because it's Christ who I will find!
I have joy and see through hope
Which looks beyond this tiny scope!"

Sister Pony's wings took flight,
And carried her above the night.
Her heart was filled with peace of course,
Because her faith had made a choice.
"I will choose to follow Christ.
I give God my very life!
His Spirit fills my heart and soul,
And makes my life grow kind and bold!
And as I pray and live His Word,
Sitting still becomes absurd!
I cannot keep it for myself!
I must share Christ with someone else!
I'll stand for more than my own life.
I'll stand for all of ponykind!
God will help me to endure,
For His love is strong and pure!"

"Come and join this pony herd,
As we enter war and serve!
You will be at peace and free,
So come along and fly with me!"

Sister Pony thought awhile,
But couldn't seem to crack a smile.
What could make her heart brand new?
There was nothing he could do!
Freedom Pony knew that look,
But it was worth the risk he took.

"Sister Pony,
you must know
About the war
over your soul.
There is an Enemy and a King-
One fights in hate, and death he brings.
But there's no need to let him win,
Because our King has beaten him!
Our King the Lord is great and strong;
The raging storms of life He calms."

Sister Pony took his hand,
And walked outside into the land.
Freedom Ponies gathered round,
And light was shining on the ground.

"Sister Pony wants to know
The victor in this violent war!
She is weak from lack of armor,
What shall we give to make her stronger?"

"The Shield of Faith will make you strong!
It will protect you from all wrong!
Sister Pony would you like
To raise this shield that brings great light?"
The shield was raised before her heart,
And she could see what once was dark.
Arrows flew with poison lies,
But faith destroyed them as she cried:
"I believe that God is great! I believe that God is strong!
I believe He loves me,
And He's there when everything seems wrong!
I live by faith and I believe
There's more to life than what I see!"

"Yes, the Shield of Faith has power,
And here's the next gift for this hour.
The Sword of Love will truly break
The foes of selfishness and hate!
Pick up the sword and you will see
How God's great love can set you free!"

Sister Pony blinked back tears.
The sword was melting deepest fears.
She raised the sword up swift and high,
And yelled these words into the night:

THE MISSION

Because there's a reason we are still here on earth.

Freedom Ponies on the loose,
Spreading tales of love and truth!
They have a gift they cannot keep,
But give away to those who seek.

Sister Pony lives next door.
She is a victim in a war.
She has little to believe,
For all she knows is what she sees.
She's never known a love that's true,
Or been accepted through and through.
As each day passes and unfolds
She wonders what the future holds.

"Hello my friend, how have you been?
I came to see you once again.
I know we've talked a lot before
About your heart that feels so sore.
Sometimes the days are full of pain,
Or in the night you feel afraid.
I've been here, to make you smile,
And trust is built for things worthwhile.
May I share something with you,
That can make your heart brand new?"

“God decided in advance to adopt us into his own family by bringing us to himself through Jesus Christ. This is what he wanted to do, and it gave him great pleasure. So we praise God for the glorious grace he has poured out on us who belong to his dear Son. He is so rich in kindness and grace that he purchased our freedom with the blood of his Son and forgave our sins.”

Ephesians 1:5-7

And so these two ponies, along with their herd,
Spend time loving others, and spreading His Word.
The change is within, for their heart is now new.
They said yes to the ultimate call and rescue.
So consider this passion. Consider this path.
The adoption is yours. Just seek, knock and ask.

Adopted!
This word.
It meant a forever.
Family, and love,
and sisters and brothers.

"Indeed it means family: and that is the Church-
All who have chosen to follow and search.
We seek Him daily, and serve in His mission
To share and call out- and speak of forgiveness."

"Forgiveness," said Freedom, and he thought of his sin.
He had guilt, he had shame. Would God adopt him?

"Forgiveness and wholeness He gives to us all,
Because of the death of His Son on the cross.
His Son paid the debt so that we would not have to.
He was punished for us:
He so loves me and you!

But He didn't stay dead! He rose from the grave!
He conquered all death! The whole world He forgave!
And He gave us His Spirit to speak to our hearts-
To comfort and draw us, and set us apart.
Father, Son, Spirit: He is the Lord!
One God, yet a family
And He calls us His His own!

Do you believe?

Do you give Him your life?

He will teach you to follow-
He will lead you to light."

"Yes, I believe!
Yes, I confess!
This news gives relief to my sorrow and stress.

To be loved as I am.
To be known through and through.
To give Him my burdens, in exchange for what's true!

I have a future, and the joy you first mentioned-
I see now... it comes from a heart that's surrendered.

I trust in my Father, He calls me His child.
He is all that I need in a world running wild."

"Stronger than tears?" Freedom stood still.
"Stronger than pain? But grief is so real."

Freedom said nothing out loud to his friend
But Courage discerned that this chat should not end.
"Joy isn't something I made for myself-
It is a gift given-
Worth far more than wealth.

Joy that endures on good days and bad.
It makes me content, even when I feel sad."
Freedom listened, a bit confused.
"Joy and grief stand together?" he thought and he mused.
Sad was what he understood.
He longed for joy: it sounded so good.

"Who gave you this gift?" Freedom said slowly,
For Courage was unaware of his story.

"My Father," said Courage,
And Freedom looked down.
Of course, she had family!
He had none to be found.

"My Father, and yours," Courage spoke up.
"Don't you know Him?" she asked.
"He's known you all your life."

Freedom's head jerked and his hair started bristling.
Was she cruel? Was it true?
He felt foolish for listening.

And Courage could see he was frightened and scared.
But the message she brought was of hope and of care.

"The Father I speak of created us all.
He is good.
He is just.
And He wants all your heart."
And it dawned on young Freedom-
this Dad who she spoke of,
Was God of creation, and King of all true love!
Wonderful Savior!
The Lord of all lords!
Father! Of course! How he longed for His voice!

"But how can I know Him?" He wondered sincerely.
"He's always been close," Courage said, bold and clearly.
"The Father has made a way for us all
To be in His family: adopted by God!"

The night was dark, the rain was cold.
He sat and shivered, all alone.

Grief so great, he wished it would stop-
He wept, and was tired.
He wailed and he fought.
Grief was a sorrow deep in his heart,
A sting so great, it pulled him apart.
He felt as if something cherished had died.
The ache wouldn't leave though he slept or he cried.
It broke his heart open till his heart felt like bleeding,
Till he shouted to God: it was God he was needing!

These were thoughts that warred within,
A heart, a mind, a soul offended.
Loss of what we hold most sacred:
It births a pain that can't be shaken.
Indeed, the pain stays with him now,
But healing did start, and this is how...

One day as he trudged through mud and through rain,
A pony walked by who seemed rather lame.
"You have a limp!" Freedom exclaimed.
"Do you need a vet? Are you in pain?"

"No, not today," Courage spoke back.
"It's just part of me. My hoof isn't flat.
I've lived this way for years and years.
I learned long ago, joy is stronger than tears."

FREEDOM PONY IS ADOPTED

FOR EVERYONE WHO NEEDS ADOPTED. TURNS OUT, THAT'S ALL OF US.

The stars above, the sea so deep.
The earth so vast, small things unique.
He thought in awe of the grandness of God,
And slowly began to sing out a song.
The song brought peace to all who would listen.
Some closed their eyes, and some eyes would glisten.
They all felt a need to be thankful too.
A sincere song of love, that bloomed and it grew.
"Who is this young horse?" you might stop and inquire.
"Why did they gather? Who did they admire?"
These are fair questions which I will now answer.
Are you ready to hear? Do not fear, though there's danger.

Freedom Pony is the horse who sang out.
He lives with a herd who all came from down south.
They spend their days playing, as most horses do.
They run in the pasture, and sometimes lose a shoe.
They eat hay or grass and visit with barn cats.
They joke and they neigh and swish tails at the rude gnats.
To you and to me it appears rather normal.
Except for the fact that it's not: I assure you.
The camaraderie here is distinctive. It's special.
A commitment runs deep: like brothers and sisters.

"Well, perhaps they are family," you nod and assume.
And they are.
But they're not.
Not the blood you presume.
They're family due to their common faith.
They've been brought together by love and by grace.
But not long ago, he was on the outside.
Alone in this world.
And lonely inside.
He had been orphaned and brought to the farm,
And this part of the story might cause you alarm.
But don't be afraid though the journey is sad,
In the end- this I promise- he will find the best Dad!

“

Dedicated to

Jesús, Alexandre, Chloé, Benjamin, Horace, Samuel, and Lou Anna.

”

Freedom Pony Fables

Freedom Pony is Adopted and The Mission

By Tina Michelle Henriot